Come
What
May

Come
What
May

Ahmed Masoud

Victorina Press
www.victorinapress.com

Typesetting and layout: Jorge Vasquez
Cover design: Clarrie-Anne Cooper

British Library Cataloguing in Publication Data
A catalogue record for this book is available from the
British Library.

ISBN: 978-1-9169057-5-7

Typeset in 11pt Garamond
Printed and bound in Great Britain by 4edge Ltd

To my mother Fatima and my sisters, Heyam, Elham, Hiba, Aida and Hind and to those who need all the strength in the world to keep going.
To the soul of my sister Bushra whom I never met.

Chapter 1

'Who cares? One more person dead, so what?'

'I do. He is . . . was my husband.'

He stared at me as though a crazy person were standing in front of him: a helpless woman begging an official to believe her – a human wreck. The look in his eyes was confusing. Was it sympathy? Disgust? Or simply boredom?

His dark olive skin appeared warm despite the cold wind outside, and his roll-neck woollen jumper reached up to meet his half grey beard, which was like a hedge growing wildly from the tip of his sideburns and his curly hair. Here was a man who didn't give much thought to his looks – unmarried maybe? His small, piercing black eyes made him appear intense. The heavy blue police jacket he was wearing was a little dusty. I wasn't sure whether he had fallen over earlier or he simply hadn't washed for a long time. There was something about his ruggedness which gave him a strong presence.

The office was almost empty, save for a long metal desk which had a square telephone and a black Dell computer screen on it. The wires trailed down to the floor where the hard drive lay flat on its side. I noticed the keyboard was white. There was a big office chair behind, tucked very close to the desk.

Nouman was sitting at the edge of the desk, next to a nameplate:

Detective Sargent Nouman El Taweel
Head of Criminal Investigation

And, as his surname suggested, he was indeed a tall man.

'Tell me, Mrs Tanani, why do you think your husband was killed?' he asked, flipping over a page of the desk calendar so it showed the current date: Tuesday 22nd December 2016.

From where we were sitting in Gaza's El Abbas police station I could hear the distant sounds of the beach.

'I don't think he was killed. I know he was . . . he's dead now.'

'Oh, yes, I am sorry. I meant murdered.'

He was looking away from me as if he didn't want to tell me what he had in mind – he didn't want to let his eyes betray him. He kept tapping the desk with three fingers, very lightly and repetitively. He did this every time he asked a question, which was incredibly distracting. I followed his gaze towards the corner of the ceiling. There were no pictures or framed Quranic verses on the walls, as was usually the case with Hamas government offices. There was a spider dangling right down to the window ledge, and Nouman was observing it intensely, waiting to see if it would travel all the way to the floor. But something made the spider stop: maybe it was listening to our conversation and eagerly awaiting my answer. I could swear it was looking at me with pity.

Nouman was typically Middle Eastern, with very well defined dark features, high cheekbones, thick lips, curly hair – all of that. If you had a remote control and paused him just before he was about to talk, you might have mistaken him for a pantomime actor. But he wasn't, he was the real thing. A lot of men in Gaza looked like that, yet he looked very special and handsome.

There was no electricity or heating in the office. The sound of wind whistled in, yet a thin sliver of sunlight broke through the thick dark clouds outside, lending a touch of brightness to the dark room. My body shivered despite the sudden appearance of the sun. The black gown on top of my short-sleeved blue top and jeans provided me with hardly any warmth. Someone on the radio had mentioned this morning that 2016 was the coldest and hottest year on record. We started the year with rain and floods, and now December wanted to finish off the year with extra freezing weather to ensure the statistics were proven correct. Or maybe it was just nature's way of washing away all the memories and pain of the dreadful wars.

'Mr Taweel, I don't think you believe my story and it seems as though I am wasting my time here.'

His eyes followed me as I gathered my stuff, lifted up the loose white headscarf which was resting on my shoulders and tightened it on my head. I could almost hear his breathing as I hurried out of the door.

Another disappointing meeting: rushing out of another office onto another cold empty street. I didn't want to stay any longer, didn't want any further humiliation, sarcastic looks, stupid questions.

There weren't many people about. A donkey cart passed by, led by a small boy of around ten years. A stray cat jumped down from a large bin filled with loosely tied plastic bags. I turned left out of the police station. Two police guards, sitting on chairs outside, wrapped in heavy coats, touched their Kalashnikovs as if getting ready for a battle. I smiled and said *Assalam Aleikom*, laughing underneath at the paranoia we lived in, at how frightened those two poor sods were of a woman who was just on her way out.

I continued walking up the hill, all the way towards the big building of the Palestinian Legislative Council, the PLC, at the top of the triangular El Rimal Public Park where the statue of the Unknown Soldier once stood. The air smelled very clean, a hint of citrus coming from a few trees in the middle of the park. An old man was roasting sweet potatoes by the side of the road. A little boy next to him was feeding the fire with twigs, and the large barbecue pot looked precarious as it rested on three big stones. But the fire and the smell of roast potatoes mixed with the citrusy air were very comforting. They brought back memories of better days: of me and Ammar before we got married; of laughing out loud on the street and being stared at by old men in suits and conservative men in *jellabiyas*. They were happy days, the kind of feeling you get on a summer holiday, a rest in between life's hectic schedules, a chance to switch off completely, waking up to warm sun on a beach somewhere, eating exotic food, meeting new people. That was what Gaza was like in the late 1990s; a city taking a break from wars, a promise that life was or could be okay.

We used to skip lectures at El Azhar University back in 1999 and walk down here as fast as we could. Once at the foot of the Unknown Soldier, we would take a few steps towards the main gate of the PLC building and make sure to see the tacky golden dome, built as a weird replica of El Aqsa Mosque in Jerusalem. Ammar would wink at me as we spotted it, then he would count to three before we split in different directions. He always took the right-hand street which led to El Shifa Hospital, past Delice Coffee Shop, while I continued straight down the hill, past El Abbas Police Station and all the way to the New Port. The aim of the game was to see who would reach the beach first.

Ammar always won the race even though his route was much longer, and apparently he never took a taxi, usually arriving without a drop of sweat on his wide forehead, no matter how hot it was. Ammar was the gentlest man any woman could wish for. He was tall with long straight hair. He never had a beard and wasn't interested in growing one. His wide brown eyes always glimmered when he smiled, which along with his dimples made him exceptionally irresistible. Unlike many Palestinian men, he wasn't hairy. In fact, far from it – he hardly had a hair on his chest.

We would sit on a big stone at El Mina El Jadeeda and watch the waves crashing into the unfinished port, discussing the lectures we had missed and wondering which of Shakespeare's lines the lecturer would have mispronounced.

***

We were both second-year students in the English department at El Azhar University in Gaza City, an institution that was born as an extension to the Mosque in Cairo, but had grown secular and was supported by Fatah, the ruling party of the Palestinian Authority at the time.

Learning Shakespeare in Gaza was hilarious – as if we didn't have enough tragedies here already, or the troubles of the kings and queens of Europe were more important. Maybe if the great writer were here he would have written different plays altogether. Maybe at least Othello would have looked slightly different and wouldn't have been referred to as a beastly Moor. If only Shakespeare had met my Ammar, he would have written about how gentle the 'Moors' are.

But the great writer was very famous in Palestine because of the endless Egyptian Arabic adaptations for theatre and screen. But I never thought I would be Prince Hamlet myself, looking at the ghost of my own murdered husband and seeking justice. I had hoped that these stories only existed on paper, not in real life, and certainly not in Gaza.

At university we studied *Henry V*, which brought hope to some of us in class that one day we would have a leader who would be able to lead the few to victory, enable the weak to grow stronger, give faith to those who had lost all hope. A leader who would bring a smile to our faces, who would look us in the eye and shout, "Once more unto the breach dear friends once more, or stop up the wall with our Palestinian dead." But instead, Yasser Arafat came along and brought with him an entourage – a corrupt band of brothers.

The Romantics took us to a faraway land, a fantasy space that could only exist in our minds. We tried to imagine what they were talking about – the green lands, the lakes, the sunsets, the trees and the daffodils. But every time we got closer to learning how they lived and what they thought about, a nearby explosion of an Israeli missile crushed our fantasy – literally. Still, we laughed at Byron's pet baby bear in Oxford, we memorised Wordsworth's words and even got excited when he mentioned Palestine in one of his poems. But the trouble with the Romantics was that they saw the world through their own eyes only. Their rich upper class view of the world meant they didn't have to worry about the stuff we cared about. They didn't have to worry about food or safety, they didn't know what it meant to wake up in the morning worrying about starving before thinking about how the 'beloved' might feel.

We hated *Robinson Crusoe* – that colonial prick was too close to home. We couldn't tolerate that imperialist propaganda, so we organised protests outside the office of the head of department, Professor Marwan. We met with the president of the university and demanded the book be removed from the curriculum. There were only five of us leading the protests, but we felt we had the intellectual and ethical responsibility to demonstrate against anything that remotely conflicted with our human rights. We asked why the university wouldn't teach us white supremacist literature about the benefits of slavery instead. The question put them to shame, and the president immediately ordered the removal of the novel from the English department's course. We won, and we celebrated by going to the British Council's office in Gaza to make a complaint about the novel being displayed on the library shelves. A month later, the book was removed.

But then we read Charles Dickens in our second year and suddenly it all became worthwhile. Studying an English Literature degree and paying high fees became worth it. The guy might as well have lived in Gaza. *Oliver Twist* broke our hearts and *Hard Times* just made us melt.

In 2000, the Second Intifada started, but we didn't care – we were lost in a different world. We didn't care that checkpoints were being erected randomly on the streets. We didn't care that a helicopter was used to bomb us in Gaza for the first time. We didn't care that so many of our friends were being killed. We didn't care that F16s started firing; that the hope for peace was dwindling; that the border was shut; that electricity was scarce; that military invasions were the norm; that each time we said goodbye to family felt like the last time we would ever say it. We didn't care because we had a world of books that was so different to everything around us, and despite the hardships in Dickens' work we were lost in wonder at what a steam engine was or what a circus looked like.

We drew pictures of what we imagined. We read passage after passage of works of geniuses to get to the twentieth century and read T S Eliot. We sat in classrooms that were full of bullet holes, pretending the bombing outside was no more than the fireworks at the circus.

***

Very often, when Ammar and I sat by the sea, we would stop laughing and – without attracting too much attention – shuffle our bums so we could get closer to each other. So close that our thighs were touching. Then our hands would melt into one, all the while looking away from each other, busy scanning the area to see if anyone had noticed, pretending we were just taking in the view. We would stroke each other's hands so gently, while staring at the glistening Mediterranean Sea ahead of us, with its gentle waves and not-so-gentle Israeli gunboats. They floated on the line where the water touched the sky, waiting to shoot any fisherman who crossed further than six miles into the sea.

When we tired of the view, we would look to the right and stare at the Mordor-like chimney exhaling thick white smoke on the other side of the fence in Asqalan port, in what's called Israel. Watching the smoke drift in small clouds towards the sea wasn't entertaining, but by that time we were often so aroused that we couldn't see anything else ahead of us. Two people in love, surrounded by gunboats, watch towers and staring conservative eyes which found our touching far more offensive than the Israeli military vessels themselves.

Our game on the way back was to see how far we could get into Gaza City while still hearing the sound of the waves. We once walked back to El Rimal Park, past Kazem's famous ice cream shop, onto the main junction of Omar El Mukhtar and El Jalaa Street, all the way up to the municipality building near El Saraya. Ammar often swore he could still hear the sound of the beach despite the noise of the street: donkeys braying; cars honking; people selling stuff, and the wonderful smell of deep fried falafel masking the stinky donkey farts as they pulled their heavily loaded carts. When I looked back at him, he was laughing, holding a seashell in his hand which he then threw at me.

'I am not lying, you see?' He started running ahead of me as if I was going to chase him and beat him up. I loved that man: he was my world. A different world that seemed far away from Palestine – a hundred light years away maybe. He wasn't normal. Everything about him took me somewhere else, away from this prison, away from destruction.

He was a dreamer. Life to him was just one big dream that he never wanted to wake up from, which made him almost oblivious to the pain and sadness surrounding him.

'So, you never threw a stone in your life? Not even a single small one at an Israeli jeep? Not one?' I once asked him as I caressed his hand, tickling his palm while reaching out to his fingertips.

'No,' he said matter-of-factly, without wanting to offer any explanation – that was it, end of story. There was no reason behind it, he didn't want to throw any stones or participate in any of the activities of the First Intifada.

'Is it true that people in Rimal District used to pick up stones with a tissue before throwing them at the soldiers and shout "Oh naughty ones, you are so horrible!"' I once asked him, but he just burst into laughter.

'I don't know, I was never there. But it's true that we Rimal City people are a bit gentler than your Jabalia Camp folks.' He laughed deeply, while I tickled his tummy for being so rude. There was something about his laughter that gave me comfort: it was innocent, long, deep. A man of such laughter was someone to trust and keep forever. Here was a man in front of me who had never thrown a stone in his life. I never thought I could be attracted to such a gentle human being.

My brothers at home always bragged about their muscles, and when we were kids they told me many stories of how they rained their stones on Israeli military jeeps. Resistance was sacred to them. There was no way to avoid talking about it in my household.

***

As I walked out of El Abbas police station on that cold day of December 22nd 2016, I remembered the joy we used to feel when we waited to see the big Christmas tree that always stood tall in the middle of El Rimal Public Park. It was donated by the government of Norway. Every year, two weeks before Christmas, the tree would be decorated with beautiful shiny baubles and empty boxes wrapped up like gifts. There was always a message underneath saying "A present to the Palestinian people from the Government of Norway." Somehow that tree was our connection to the outside world – it made us part of it.

But since 2007, when Hamas took over Gaza and Israel imposed a heavy siege on this Strip, a tree hasn't been sent. Maybe the Norwegians knew that not even Santa Claus or God could break through the Israeli siege, so they saved themselves the money and embarrassment.

Today, I walked back home alone, with no tree to look

at and no Ammar to hold on to. My head was heavy, thinking of who could have murdered him. Why would anyone do that? Two years and five months had passed but it felt like it was only yesterday that Ammar left home and never returned.

The smell of sweet potatoes made me very hungry. I touched my stomach while walking past the Bank of Palestine, and took the second right, up another small hill until I got to Talatini Street. I turned left and walked all the way past the Islamic University of Gaza and the UN Headquarters where Ammar used to work as a translator. But just before I reached the front door of our building, a police car pulled up to the side of the road. Mr. Nouman got out and waved to the driver to go.

'Zahra, could I have a word please?'

Chapter 2

Although it was only 1 p.m. it was getting dark outside, as more grey clouds gathered. The entrance of the four storey building was almost pitch black; the electricity switch was useless with the lack of power. I ushered Mr. Nouman inside and felt my way up the three steps at the start of the hallway as we continued up the stairs to my two-bed, first-floor flat. Mr. Nouman followed me in silence as I led us both through the brown wooden door and into the living room. I went straight to the kitchen to make some bitter black coffee, stirring hard, letting the heat from the hob seep into my palms. Making coffee on that cold afternoon was very comforting and the aroma of the cardamom-infused drink filled the whole kitchen.

It was strange to have a man sitting in the living room. Not many people had come to visit me for a long time and certainly not an attractive man. I put the coffee and two small cups on a round metal tray along with a glass of water and returned to the living room. Mr. Nouman turned his face away as soon as I bent down to serve him his cup. My top buttons had come undone while taking off my long black gown in the kitchen and the curve of my breasts was showing.

'Don't worry, I'm not trying to seduce you. I just like to be comfortable in my home.'

An awkward silence filled the place. I was expecting him to leave any minute. He sipped his coffee very quickly and returned it to the tray. Then he took the glass of water and drank it all in one gulp.

'I would like to look into your case,' he said. My eyes began to water and before I could do anything the warm liquid started falling down my cheeks. I caught some of the tears in the corner of my mouth as I smiled.

Opening the small drawer in the coffee table, I took out a packet of Royals cigarettes, lit one with a match and puffed out a sigh of relief, considering what to say next. I continued to smoke as I stared at the sofa with glittery edges which Ammar and I had bought together.

'Smoking is not good for you.'

'Anything that speeds up death in this godforsaken concentration camp is welcome.' He looked at me strangely after I said that. Maybe he wasn't comfortable being with a woman in her own home, her top buttons open as she smoked a cigarette. Maybe I pushed my luck with him a little. After all, he was a Hamas policeman.

'What made you change your mind?' I asked, flicking the ash from my cigarette into the palm of my hand, not bothering to stand up and fetch an ashtray. He looked at me as if offended by the question.

'Hmm . . . let's just say I like complicated cases, Mrs. Tanani.'

'Please call me Zahra.'

'Or um . . . children? A son I could call you a mother of?'

'No children . . . yes, thirty-four years old and no children. We never wanted any, but now I wish we had. Having a child gives you a reason to live, it makes you selfless and self-obsessed at the same time. You think about someone else but you would like to believe they're the best in the world. The reality is that they're just spoiled brats. But I wish I had one now, it would distract me a little.'

'Tell me, Zahra, why are you so convinced Ammar was murdered? Why can't you accept it was the same Israeli attack that killed him and the people with him in the house in Shujaia?'

'He had a stab wound . . . and he didn't go to Shujaia that night. He had no reason to be there. He phoned me on my mobile shortly before he was killed saying he was in El Saha and he would be home soon.'

The taste of my tears felt disgusting as I swallowed them back, not wanting to show Nouman my weakness.

'But the body was found in a house in Shujaia with four others – two men and two women?'

'Yes,' I replied quickly.

'So, you are saying someone stabbed Ammar with a knife, carried the body from El Saha and dumped it in a house full of martyrs from an Israeli bombshell?'

'Well . . . yes . . . though maybe not if you put it that way.'

Nouman crossed his legs as he leant back on the sofa.

'Do you smoke?' I asked nervously as I refilled his cup of coffee from the pot.

'No, thanks.'

'Does Hamas ban you from smoking then?' I tried to lighten the atmosphere with a joke. He looked at me, surprised by the question. There was a hint of disgust in the way he stared.

'As a matter of fact, I am not Hamas, never have been, never will be. Or Fatah for that matter. I am not politically affiliated. My job is to catch criminals. I did it when Fatah was in power and even when the Israelis were running this Strip. I investigate murders, that's all, okay?'

The sharpness of his tone made me worried that he might change his mind about taking on my case.

'Now we've cleared that one up, let me tell you that I am not finding your story entirely convincing. Can you imagine the trouble someone would have to go to in order to stab someone to death, then carry their body in the middle of an Israeli massacre through Shujaia Town as everyone was trying to leave? An Israeli soldier was captured that night and the Israelis responded by flattening the entire neighbourhood. Think – does this make sense to you?'

'No,' I replied nervously, all the while looking down at the dusty floor.

'Well?' He smiled.

'The post mortem confirmed that he was the only one with stab wounds. He did not look like he was killed by shrapnel.'

My tears now started to fall uncontrollably. I was back to square one here, having explained this to everyone a thousand times.

'The stab wound could have been a result of shrapnel, or he might have fallen on something. I don't think we can start a whole murder investigation based on this. If, as you claim, your husband wasn't in Shujaia at the time of his murder, what was he doing in El Saha then?'

At least he was asking some questions, and his fingers were tapping the sofa.

'He was having *shisha* in El Saha with some friends.'

'Mrs. Tanani, please, have some respect for my intelligence here. Are you trying to convince me that your husband went to meet friends and smoke *shisha* with his mates in the middle of a war zone, while the Israelis were bombing the shit out of Shujaia, which is only a ten-minute drive from El Saha in the centre of Gaza City. Just to clarify, we are talking about the 19th July 2014, not any other night?'

'Yes . . . why don't you believe me?'

'I'm not saying I don't, but in my opinion it is a strange and stupid thing to have done.'

He continued to look at me, waiting for my response, but there was no response to give him. The only thing I wanted to do was go to my bedroom and lie down, close my eyes and wish that none of this had happened. It wasn't easy to re-live that evening, to start blaming myself again for not stopping him from going out, for not cooking a nice meal, for not hiding in our bedroom and having endless sex, accompanied by the drum roll of Spitfires bombing everything around us while the sound of drones added an endless buzzing noise.

I gave up. I had never been questioned this closely

about Ammar. Maybe everyone was right, maybe he was just collateral damage. Maybe no one would believe the burning feeling inside me that he was murdered.

'Ammar's behaviour in his last days was very strange. There was a lot happening I didn't understand. I had never seen my husband like that. He was worried about something—'

'The damn war, perhaps,' Nouman interrupted.

'Yes . . . no, not that. In fact, he wasn't the least bit worried about the war. He shut himself away from it completely – as if it wasn't there. But something else was troubling him. Often he would wake up in the middle of the night, shouting. He would say names that I had never heard of; he would be gasping for breath.'

I looked at the detective, pleading with him to believe me.

'So, you think he had enemies?'

'Enemies? I am not sure I would go that far, but I think something was going on that I didn't know about.'

'You need to come to the police station again so we can open a case for you and start the official procedures. I am free next Tuesday if you would like to drop by. But for now, could I please have a look around the flat? I am assuming this is where you and Ammar lived?'

My goodness, he was still interested. He hadn't given up! Mr. Nouman wanted to open the case for me at the police station.

'Yes, of course, by all means. Just give me a minute, though. I was out all morning and I haven't checked the status of the flat. I would have to kill myself if you saw my underwear.'

After quickly removing the washing-up from the sink and putting it in the fridge, I ran to my room and shoved the clothes under the bed, frantically throwing my bras into the big white wardrobe, then shouted for Nouman to come through.

His footsteps sounded heavy, almost as if counting how many steps it took him to get from the living room. I met him by the door of the kitchen; he was touching the side walls as he walked. He looked through everything, counted the dishes, the pans, and made notes of what he saw. I watched him as he breathed heavily, bending down to check the gas cooker on top of the kitchen surface. Then he touched the red hose and followed it down to the blue gas cylinder with the name 'Ammar Bseiso' written on it. He looked at the wall next to the fridge and trailed it all the way back to the door.

'You need to get this wall checked; you've got a leak somewhere and it is going mouldy.'

I smiled, not knowing what to say – a mouldy wall was the last thing on my mind. Nouman went out of the kitchen and turned right.

He politely asked to enter the bedroom. He stopped by the door and looked around the entire room. I felt I had to leave him to it rather than just stand there watching his every move. Besides, I was bored with looking through my dull things again. Walking back to the living room, I remembered how much I missed having a man in the bedroom. It had been a while. Ammar used to take his time fixing his hair and doing up his shirt. He would spend almost forty-five minutes in front of the mirror, just putting gel in his hair or aftershave. He used to whistle a lot, songs of Um Kalthoum, Abdel Halim Hafiz, and sometimes Kazem El Saher. As if he were in a Hollywood film, Nouman started humming Hafez's song, 'Ala Hisb-Widad'. My body shivered as I remembered how much Ammar loved that song and how he used to whistle the tune while sitting in the bedroom. I wanted Nouman to stay there – hum, sing, whistle, do whatever he liked.

But panic crept over me like a malignant vine. What if someone knocked on the door now? What if one of my brothers dropped by suddenly? They would beat the hell out of me and worse, I would be forced to move back to the family house in Jabalia Camp and no longer be allowed to stay here on my own, in the place Ammar and I made together. I didn't know what to do, the only thing I could think of was to join in the whistling and sway my body, dancing away all my fear. I was risking everything a widowed woman living on her own in Gaza could: her hard earned independence from a conservative society, the possibility of having a detective on her side, and an attractive man taking offence at her action.

I closed my eyes and imagined Nouman walking over and holding me from behind as Ammar used to do, telling me how much he loved me, then teasing me about something. But that moment of serenity didn't last long. It stopped as soon as the humming did, and then Nouman was back in the front room.

'Okay, I am done now,' he said, as if he was some kind of plumber who had just finished doing a paid job.

'Oh, okay. You can stay for tea if you like,' I said desperately.

'No, Mrs. Tanani, thank you, but I dare not imagine what the neighbours are now thinking about you having a man humming in the bedroom. I apologise for that.'

'Oh don't worry, please, the neighbours don't have a high opinion of me anyway.'

He stared at me as I said this; I felt very embarrassed. There was something in his eyes which gave me the impression he understood what I meant, that he knew all about the visits from the neighbours after Ammar died – to tell me to get married again, to explain that a woman's honour needs to be maintained otherwise people 'will talk'. It's almost as if he understood the look on our neighbour's face every time a sales person knocked on the door. She wanted to see if it was a suitor, and waited on the staircase to eavesdrop without even making an effort to hide herself. Nouman's look gave me the impression that he knew all about the men on the street who always responded to anything I said with *"Allah*

Yoster Aleiki?', God protect your honour, as if I were some loose woman, some degenerate human being. And as he stood there in front of me, I still wasn't sure whether he was like all those other men or not.

'I must be off now, I will see you next Tuesday at my office at the police station,' he said as he put his shoes on and opened the front door.

'One more question though . . . I . . . er, didn't see any photos of Ammar anywhere? Why is that?'

The question took me aback, I wasn't expecting it.

'Never mind,' he said, breaking the silence, 'please bring a photograph with you when you come to the office. *Assalam Aleikom.*'

And with that he was gone, down the dark stairs. I rushed to the balcony to see if he looked back towards the flat, but he hurried down Talateeni street, hailed a cab, and a girl dressed in a long *jilbab* gown and white scarf opened the door and got out of the car to let him in. I assumed another man was sitting on the other side and she didn't want to be sandwiched between the two of them, as was often the habit of conservative girls in Gaza when using shared taxis.

As the old 90s Peugeot sped down the streets, a weird feeling of both relief and worry came over me. Finally, after two years of searching for someone to help me find out what had happened, a detective was taking me seriously. Yet Mr. Nouman had something about him that made me worry. I hurried inside and shut the door behind me, wondering whether I had just opened a floodgate. And it was only then, as I sat on the sofa, when a sensation came over me; a tingling in my body, a joyful happiness from having a man singing in my bedroom. I lay down on the sofa and curled up as I whistled 'Ala Hisb-Widad'.

One of the things that Palestinian men – particularly those from Gaza – had that not many in the Arab World – or elsewhere – had, was an exceptionally round bottom.

Ammar had a wonderful round bottom, but Nouman's was far rounder and tighter, even though the man was in his fifties – almost eighteen years older than me.

I whistled away, a wide smile on my face, and thought about how attractive my detective was.

But I also felt extremely guilty to be fantasising about the man who was investigating my husband's death. I got up and went to the bathroom to wash my face, cursing myself for having such ideas, feeling like someone who had just masturbated for the first time.

Chapter 3

The next Friday, I went back home to Jabalia Camp. I walked all the way down to Talatini Street, then to El Saha, instead of taking a taxi. The weather was nice and the sun warmed the damp, cracked walls. The smell of sand slowly warming up in the sun was so strong that it made me sneeze. There were very few people on the street and fewer cars than usual. Friday was a sit-at-home day for a lot of people; a perfect strolling day for a woman like me who did not conform to being all covered up. I passed the white municipality building and reached the main square of the city, and a taxi driver waiting by the statue of the lower jaw of a phoenix asked me if I was going to Jabalia Camp. I nodded and followed him while staring at the weird sculpture.

I always found it annoying that we didn't have a proper public transport system in Gaza. Instead, we had to use shared taxis, which had fixed pick-up points but could drop you anywhere en route. If we wanted them to divert, then that was a special taxi order, which was more expensive.

***

Ammar and I walked here many times on hot summer evenings, eating *tormos* beans as we circled the square. He had a favourite spot in Falasteen Café on the third floor, opposite the branch of the Arab Bank. We used to go to the corner of the balcony where he always ordered the same watermelon flavoured *shisha* to smoke.

'Legend has it that the symbol of Gaza is a phoenix,' he would say as he stared down at the statue, as if wanting to jump all the way down to ride it.

'Because Gaza rebuilds itself every time it gets destroyed,' he added, while exhaling a huge cloud of smoke. There was a look in his eyes that suggested he almost wanted to believe that nonsense. Maybe deep down he had some political interest which he never allowed himself to share with me.

'Well, if this is what they mean by 'rebuild itself', then I prefer ashes.' My attempt to dismiss the idea wasn't very successful.

'Hayati, you are sitting at a crossroad in this Strip, where Africa meets Asia, where civilisations collide, where blood has been spilt, emperors have fallen, princes married. This place belongs to history. Don't write it off just yet! Even Alexander the Great besieged this shithole for months, and when he won he killed all the men and sold the women and children as slaves.'

He was talking as though he was giving a history class to a bunch of school kids, proud of his knowledge and waiting for questions from the bewildered audience. He gazed through me as he handed me the *shisha* hose to smoke – an act which many Palestinian men in Gaza would find disgraceful. Of course, many women smoked *shisha*, a lot of them without their husband's knowledge, but for the majority, it was not okay to smoke *shisha* in public. Some people said that Hamas banned women from doing so, but that was never true. Men who were a little paranoid about their masculinity followed the rumours blindly and, like many things in this dungeon, rumours quickly became rules.

We smoked, talked, and imagined ourselves able to travel to Cairo for a visit: walk down the famous Nile; eat some famous Egyptian Kouchari on the Corniche of the mighty river. We pictured ourselves like any other couple in the world, planning holidays and escapes and getting excited by the idea of being away from everyone we knew. Neither of us had travelled out of Gaza before, but we had heard stories about the trip from the Rafah border, down the south of Gaza, all the way through the Sinai desert, crossing the October Bridge over the Suez Canal. We had never seen a desert before. We argued sometimes about whether it would look like those Jordanian Bedouin soap operas, where there was a Sheikh, a leader of a certain clan, living in a huge luxurious tent and normally trying to avenge the murder of some of his tribesmen. And, of course, there was always a love story involving a beautiful young woman covered with tattoos, dressed in a long wide gown showing parts of her shoulders, often matching the colour of her Gazelle-like eyes. Her beloved was always a good horse rider, wearing a long brown gown on top of his white *jellabiya*, with either a gun or a dagger attached to his belt.

We laughed as we imagined ourselves walking into one of those Bedouin tents, wondering whether they even existed in real life.

***

Now, as I followed the driver to his taxi near the statue, I looked up and noticed that Falasteen Café had closed down. The big sign that used to hang on the balcony had disappeared, leaving only peeling paint visible. We kept walking, until we got to the Sanada area, where the driver had parked. The engine was still running, puffing dark clouds of smoke which stank of cheap petrol. There were three men in the car already and they were relieved to see me and to know they had their fourth passenger, meaning their journey could begin. With the lack of buses in Gaza, car owners did very well in transforming their vehicles into shared taxis. I could have taken a private taxi for myself and gone all the way down to Jabalia Camp. But sharing a cab with others made me feel somehow normal – that I still was a human being in that city, wanting the same things they wanted, using the same old cars and pretending that life was the usual routine.

Despite the fumes coming out of the exhaust pipe, I kept the window rolled down and enjoyed the cold breeze on my face. But deep down, I was worried about how to inform my family of the news that I had found a detective who'd agreed to take on the case. I was sure my brother Jamil would give me a hard time.

I leant out of the window and watched as the driver sped down the Sanada, onto Yaffa Street and then to Masoud Street in the heart of Jabalia town. The smell of orange and lemon trees started to penetrate my nose as we passed a couple of small farms before turning left towards El Juron, and then right, straight to Jabalia Camp. The thirty-minute drive took us only fifteen minutes this time, as the streets were quiet, due to the Friday prayer already being underway.

I had just noticed that the guy sitting next to me in the middle of the back seat of the taxi was keeping as far away from me as possible – almost leaning on the other guy's lap. He had prayer beads in his hands and was praying to God for forgiveness because he had sat next to a woman. I had to resist the urge to sit on his lap. In that moment I suddenly realised I had more power than those bearded men, that they were scared more of us women than we were of them, that the threat of going to hell for sitting next to a woman in a car was really a powerful weapon. I was relishing this moment, wanting to test it more. But the trouble was that I was scared he would get violent, as was often the case. He was a large bloke and I didn't want to be beaten up, spat at or be pushed out of the car. I had never seen anything like this happen in front of my eyes, but men scared me, especially those who believed God told them to treat women like that. But women here can only be empowered when they're either old or divorced and ostracised from society.

The Camp was quiet too, as we passed the Khadamat Jabalia Sports Club, headed down to El Markez and right up to Trans Road where my family lived. My two brothers, Issa and Jamil, were out at the mosque when I got in. Mother was sitting in the kitchen on a small stool. A big tray in front of her with flour on it made me realise that *maftoul* was on the menu for lunch. My mouth started to water as I watched her dig her thick hands into the dough mixture, adding small amounts of salt and water, then holding some in her palms and rolling it hard so that the couscous got smaller and smaller. She looked so hot, despite the chilly weather. She smiled as I entered, but couldn't get up to hug me or shake my hands, as she was covered in white flour. Three of my nephews and nieces came running into the kitchen and nearly fell over Mother's big tray. Their two mothers came chasing after them and shouted at them to leave, threatening to tell Issa and Jamil when they returned from the mosque. They smiled as they saw the chocolate coming out of my pockets, ran towards me, gave me a big hug and quickly grabbed the sweets before their mothers could tell them off. They were out of the kitchen in a flash.

My two sisters-in-law were young and conservative. They talked about nothing except housework, the price of things, shopping, and their husbands' work. They found me and my Gaza City lifestyle of little interest; in fact, the whole family didn't approve of my staying in the same flat that Ammar and I had bought together. They wanted me to move back with them to the four-bedroom house in Jabalia Camp, where Mother and my brothers and their families lived. Father had passed away a long time ago, so we had all learned to respect Issa, the eldest of my two brothers, as a father figure for all of us. For my brothers it was out of the question that a woman would live on her own in Gaza, and they felt ashamed and angry. They avoided the subject every time neighbours or someone from the extended family asked them about it. I, on the other hand, held my ground, and managed to stay put by promising that I would move back soon. My brothers oversaw the family affairs, I had no say.

***

Father died on my 14th birthday; I was born on 21st March 1981, hence why the name Zahra was given to me. The full name was Zahrat El Rabie – spring flower. Only dad called me by my full name, while Mother and my brothers only used Zahra. Father also said that I was a gift to his wife, as I was born on Mother's Day.

Father died on 21st March 1995, and my birthday and the arrival of spring became meaningless ever after – I never celebrated either of them.

They brought him back in a large wooden coffin, which was open. His eyes were closed. He was lifted onto a big truck, with a crowd of people standing on it, holding the rails. As is tradition, they brought him home to be washed and wrapped in his white shroud. He was laid in the bath. Issa didn't want us to come inside, but I couldn't just stand outside. I walked in immediately without listening to my brother's orders. I washed my father: his face, his legs, the scars on his chest from the cancer operation. I kissed him. The more I rubbed his body, the more my tears fell on him, but without making a sound. He was the only man who never hit me, who never shouted at me, who stopped Jamil from beating me, who taught me chess, played football with me. He was the man who bought me two dresses for Eid; the man who never came to my school to ask the teachers how I was doing and just took my word for it; the man who taught me love. I was his only daughter and he knew how to love me and make me feel special all the time.

I kept washing, scrubbing and crying. Mother came into the bathroom and pulled me out. It was time to let go; they were going to take him away, put him in a small hole in the ground in the Eastern Graveyard just near the fence with Israel. Only the men were allowed to go and lay him down in his final resting place.

Issa and Jamil were already grown up when Father died. Issa had graduated from university and was working as a maths teacher in the local UN Refugee School. At the age of twenty-one, he was already married with one son, Zuheir, named after my father. Jamil quit studying and worked as an apprentice with Uncle Emad in his blacksmith workshop. When he was nineteen, he married Uncle's daughter, Basma. He was their boy, really. Uncle had eight daughters but no son, and he treated Jamil as his own. Mother was never happy about how absent Jamil was from the house and the way Uncle's wife always talked about him as her own child during family gatherings. Jamil was conservative and liked to follow traditions. So when he knew that I was going out with Ammar during the first year of university, he was furious, shouting at me and telling Issa to ban me from going to classes completely, arguing that I brought nothing but disgrace to the family name. Issa was very angry too and he didn't allow me to go for a few days, but I was never banned from going entirely. They both promised that if I continued to see Ammar they would marry me off to the first person who asked for my hand. It was frightening but flattering somehow; it felt as though I were in a fairy tale.

When Ammar came to propose to me during the final year of our studies in 2002, everyone was surprised. They really did believe that we had stopped seeing each other. Issa felt betrayed, avoiding Jamil's accusing looks, as if saying 'told you so'. Being the father figure in the family, Issa still had to offer the best hospitality to the guests, yet Jamil continued to murmur offensive words about how badly behaved Ammar was and how he took other people's daughters for a ride. When Ammar's father formally asked for my hand for his son, Jamil instantly stood up.

'Our family rules don't allow us to marry into Gaza City people. We are refugees in your city and we will go back to our homes at some point when Palestine is liberated,' he shouted as he left the room.

Issa had to control the situation and told the guests we needed some thinking time, asking them to check in a week, as was the custom. I got a slap or two when Issa asked me whether I had continued seeing Ammar or not. There was no point in lying. We loved each other. There was no way that either of us could be with anyone else. Neither of my brothers talked to me for a few days and Mother only exchanged the bare minimum of words with me. Yet although they didn't allow her to speak to me either, there was sympathy in her eyes. She felt sorry for me. She knew how much I missed Father and wanted him to be there to save Daddy's girl from this humiliation.

My brothers were also aware of the social difference between our two families. Ammar's was the true Gazan, upper class family that had lived in the Gaza Strip for hundreds of years, and my family was a small, poor peasant family from Palestine, kicked out of our village of Herbia in 1948, which the Israelis had renamed Seidrot. Our family knew a great deal about farming citrus fruits and very little about anything else. Ammar's family were the sophisticated well-educated city people who kept Gaza alive with trade and culture for generations. You couldn't hear the surname Bseiso being mentioned without thinking of the famous poet Mu'in Bseiso, or Atef Bseiso, the PLO official who was killed by Israel, or Sakhar Bseiso, the former governor of Gaza. The family name would be intimidating to any other refugee girl and stop any romance from flourishing.

Being confined to the house for a few days, things became unbearable for me and my sisters-in-law. We argued about everything, until Ammar's father rang on the Friday. Issa answered the phone. I only heard, '*Inshallah*, come this evening and we will discuss.' Then, without even looking at me, he said, 'Get yourself ready, you are getting engaged tonight.'

I really didn't know what changed his view that Friday. He wanted me to be happy, he always had, but he never told me what changed his mind. Maybe he recognised love; maybe he knew it was hopeless for him to try and stop us.

**

Today, as I came home, thirteen years later, all alone and my mind filled with questions about Nouman, I wished that none of this had happened.

Jamil came home from the mosque first and gave me a look of disgust.

'Can't you city folks learn how to dress modestly? At least when you come to a conservative refugee camp,' he whispered, as we embraced.

'What's wrong with what I am wearing now? It's just jeans, and the black gown covers everything, no one can see my body *wallah*!' Swearing by God's name didn't help much. He let go of me and bent down to pick up his three-year-old daughter, Ayya, who was down by his knees, nagging to be carried.

'I blame Hamas for allowing you to dress like this in Gaza City,' he said, as he carried his daughter away.

'Well, I blame Hamas for a lot of other things too,' I quipped. I could swear I saw a smile underneath that straight face but he would not admit to it. He just turned and left the room, singing a beautiful lullaby to his daughter – the very same one my father used to sing to me.

> *Nami Nami Ya Segheira, sleep sleep oh little one*
> *Ta Nirba Aal Hasira, so we can grow up on the matt*
> *Bukra beik Jaye, tomorrow your father will return*
> *Carrying cash from the lemon harvest*
> *So he can buy a new dress*
> *To keep you warm in January.*

During lunch, when we all sat crouched on the floor in the main guest room, furnished with Arabic-style mattresses, cushions and a warm Persian rug, Mother started by asking Issa who he had seen at the mosque. She questioned him about paying the debt to Abu Yehya, the corner shop owner, and whether he had called Tayseer the plumber.

Jamil became suddenly angry.

'I will fix the leak in the bathroom,' he said, without even looking at anyone, in between stuffing his mouth with *maftoul* grains and hot chicken. The steam was still coming out of his mouth even after he swallowed.

'You keep talking, but nothing ever happens,' Mother smiled, as she threw a big piece of chicken which landed on my tray, sending a few couscous grains flying in the air.

That was one of the many funny ways Mother showed her affection to me, acknowledging my presence with generosity; as if concerned only for my well-being. Everything else was just noise. I loved that woman. Oh, how I wished she would move to live with me in Gaza City and leave my two brothers to their own wives. But she wouldn't – all her friends were in the Camp and she found it difficult to move.

'I've found a detective who will investigate Ammar's case. His name is Nouman El Taweel and he's based in El Abbas Police Station in Gaza City. We will be opening an official case this Tuesday.'

I wanted to say it as quickly as possible without any interruption from anyone and, as I expected, Jamil's anger was uncontrollable. He pushed dishes of food upside down, spilling cups of Fanta on the carpet. He even pushed his wife away from him, for no apparent reason. My head was lowered and I couldn't lift it to look at him. I half expected some random cup or plate to fly towards me and hit me directly on the head. Issa shouted at him to be quiet, using his most authoritative father figure voice.

'But why? We discussed this a thousand times over! Why

can't she just accept it and let it go, move back to Jabalia Camp and we will find her a new husband?!' Jamil pressed his lips tightly together as if trying not to say anything further.

'Marry a man with two other wives and ten children, so she can end up the cleaner and housekeeper?' Mother shouted at him.

'Her husband is dead, dead, dead . . . Do you understand? It doesn't matter whether it was an Israeli jet, drone, bullet or some other fucker who killed him. The point is he is dead. And now we are disgraced by this girl who has been roaming Gaza with no shame whatsoever, walking alone at night and even sleeping rough on the streets. What she needs is a psychiatrist, not a detective. She is mentally ill. If Father was alive, he would not have this.'

As soon as he finished his sentence, Issa, who was much larger than him, jumped on him and pushed him down, so he was lying on his back on the mattress. Issa put his knee on Jamil's chest and pressed hard.

'Say this one more time and you will be dead. Are you saying that your sister is a whore? Shame on you. Get out of my sight, right now!'

Issa pushed Jamil away and shouted at him to leave the room. Jamil left, staring at me and murmuring swear words as he walked out. Mother watched in silence. She let it happen, and for some reason did not interfere between the two brothers; instead she simply stood up and left the room herself. So did Issa and his wife, Samar. Jamil's wife, Basma, stood up and began to clear up. I leant back against the wall and held my knees with my hands, bringing them closer to my chest. The room was full of dirty dishes and there were grains everywhere. An ant crawled on the plastic sheet that covered the carpet. It took one grain of *maftoul* and carried it away. I wondered what this ant was doing outside in winter. Was it too lazy to work over summer and hadn't stored enough for the winter? Or was it simply as lonely as I was and didn't give a flying monkey's about what others thought while it was out?

I thought of Father and wished he were there. Would he really be disgraced by my trying to find the truth? Didn't he always tell me to speak the truth even if it cost me everything? Why was Jamil so adamant to stop me from finding out? What was it that offended him so much? The idiot had helped me without realising. He had dented Issa's dignity. I smiled as a thought came to my head – Issa hadn't said no and his word was the one I had to worry about. He was the father in the family and now I had his consent. I was determined to find my husband's killer, come what may.

Chapter 4

'Her husband is dead, dead, dead.'

Jamil's voice kept ringing in my ear, haunting every single thought I had about what to say to Nouman when we next met. Why was it so difficult for people to understand that I needed to find out what had happened to my husband? Why did they get so offended? It was none of their business anyway.

But doubt crept into my mind. On Sunday, I took a long walk down to the big Omari mosque in Gaza City. With every step, doubt was turning into fear, which itself was turning into depression. Tuesday couldn't come soon enough to see my detective. The idea of dropping it altogether and running away was very tempting. Luckily, Gaza was under siege and there was nowhere to escape to – meeting Nouman was the inevitable thing to do.

The quietness of Gaza at night was no different from that of a jail at midnight, when the lights were switched off and the prisoners were made to sleep. Like a prisoner, I too slept every night, ticking off one day at a time – not off my sentence, but off my life.

***

When I arrived on Tuesday, Nouman was sitting behind his desk on the black chair. He had lots of papers in front of him, old folders with rusty metal binders in them. There were A4 pictures of what looked like dead people, all black and white. Some even fell on the floor as the detective moved his hands quickly to the keyboard of the computer to type something.

'Can I smoke here?' I asked nervously. He stood up, opened the window, let the cold breeze in, then looked at me.

'Go ahead, kill yourself, be my guest.'

The detective's voice wasn't patronising, it was deep and comforting, and he almost sounded disappointed that I still hadn't taken notice of his advice to give up smoking. But the addiction was far greater than any responsible thoughts. He watched me exhale lungfuls of smoke – for a moment I thought he liked it. But then he pretended to cough and smiled.

'Okay, I need you to continue smoking that cancer piece and think hard. Go back to that night of the 19th July, close your eyes if you wish. I want you to describe to me exactly what happened – everything you know, please. Names, places, times, anything you can remember would be helpful.'

He opened his small notebook, flipped over a page and held his Parker pen in his left hand, ready to take notes. I watched him for a moment or two, then closed my eyes while puffing clouds of smoke, feeling his gaze on me.

'We had spent the first two weeks of the war in the flat. Ammar did not want to go out at all. As soon as the war started and the missiles began falling everywhere, Ammar went out shopping and bought lots of food. He ran to Abu Hussam's shop at the end of the street and got large bags of rice, canned food, vegetables, a box of bottles of Coca Cola, seeds and mixed nuts, and – of course – more cigarettes for me. He also bought lots of batteries for the handheld radio, to use when the power was off, and lined up loads of films to watch. Everything was on the menu, except one thing – the news. Ammar called his mother, Enass, on her mobile and spoke to her only to make sure that everyone was okay. She regularly gave him the updates about Tel El Hawa neighbourhood: who had been killed and what buildings had been destroyed; who was injured; who was missing. But my husband never listened, he just muttered 'aha, aha' and said a few *hamdellahs* or *Allah Yerhamhoms* out of respect for the dead every now and again.'

'And he kept his cool during that period? How?'

I suddenly realised that my eyes were still shut; when I opened them Nouman was staring at me intensely. Hearing the detective's voice shook me out of my daydream. It had just occurred to me that for some reason no one had asked me that question before – not even my mother. Yes, how did Ammar keep his cool during that time? How could we have stayed in one place that could have been torn to pieces so easily by a bomb? I never questioned it myself – yes, I was scared initially, but it all changed after the first week of the war. It became normal, almost like living near train tracks. We learned to zone out the noise outside.

'I don't know how, but we did. We ate a lot, watched TV, played cards, had lots of sex – it was fun in parts, scary in others. I can't really describe it in simple words. Every time a bomb fell, the whole apartment shook. There was that moment of vibration when we watched things hanging on the wall fall down. We felt it right there, in the stomach, held on to whatever was closest to us and waited for the sound of ambulances and police sirens to follow. Very often, more than one bomb would fall, and as they rained down people would be screaming, babies crying. But we just stared at each other, in oblivion. Every time the bombing intensified, we did not know whether we were ever going to witness another round or not. To start with, I didn't understand why Ammar wanted to stay in. But by the second week of the war, it all made sense. There was nowhere for us to go, nothing was safe; UN schools were being bombed, hospitals, mosques and residential apartments in the middle of Gaza City. Ammar wanted us to stay in our home and to face our death there, rather than anywhere else. One day, a bomb fell and completely destroyed an eight-storey building right next to us. Our apartment felt like it was swaying, I was in a daze, unsure what was happening. My ears were ringing; I thought I had gone deaf. Then, suddenly, I felt something I had only experienced once before. When I was younger, I nearly drowned in the sea. I was on the beach making sandcastles. I wanted to get some water in my plastic bucket to fill in the moat I had built around my art piece. A big wave came and pulled me into deep water. I was only nine years old and could hardly swim. I started to swallow mouthfuls of salty water while shouting. But then, everything became still. There was silence all around me; I was swaying with the wave but couldn't feel any pain or hear any splashing. It was comforting somehow. I opened my eyes and smiled as I saw the sun glittering on the surface of the water. My head was heavy as I sank, but I wasn't concerned. I was relaxed. Then I felt a hand on my shoulder and the next thing I knew I was back on the sand – my brother Issa towering over me. I coughed, and a torrent of water came out.

'By the second week of the war, every bomb gave me that very same feeling, making me sink with the waves, but this time, they were sound ones. It was a beautiful feeling to let go and just enjoy the ride – sometimes holding Ammar's hand.'

'That sounds romantic,' Nouman was smiling, but looking down at his notebook. 'Tell me – did he not even speak to friends?'

'Some, a few text messages here and there.'

'Who to?' Nouman interrupted.

'Not sure.'

'Hmm . . . strange,' he said as he flipped the page and cleared his throat. 'Don't you find this a little strange? I was going crazy during the war. I made sure I called everyone twice a day. I listened to the news on the radio, read it on the internet, watched it on TV. It's what people do – they want to know about each other.'

'But what for? That's what my husband said, the first time

I said exactly the same thing to him. "When you die you die, it doesn't make a difference who is still alive and who isn't, the same works if someone else dies. If it doesn't matter to them, why should it matter to me? Let's sit here and enjoy ourselves, come what may." That was always his response. The longer the war continued, the more I got into it and saw his point of view. We didn't turn into cave people or anything like that and we made occasional appearances on the street. We had a big balcony just outside our bedroom and we sat there for much of the time, chatting politely to the neighbours and drinking too much coffee. It was only at night when we retreated to our homemade audio theatre, where we just braced ourselves for another long night of shaking.'

Nouman stopped writing; he was staring at me. I had nothing to add to this, only my pain, but how could I show him that? How could I scream in front of this detective, and tell him that despite all that monstrous war, for us things were different? That we blocked it out completely? The war had ceased to become our entertainment – it simply vanished. We could no longer hear the sound of machine guns, explosions and rockets flying in and out of Gaza. We no longer heard the sound of sirens on the streets, and we stopped talking to anyone who mentioned the subject or had a political theory about how the war would end.

A great trait of my lovely people in Gaza was that they always had a theory of some kind and they were not afraid to share it. A baker would normally have a theory about engineering and how it all worked; the engineer, in turn, would surely have a theory about art. And whenever there was a big Israeli assault on Gaza, everyone in the Strip became a political analyst, they would follow every report and every expert on Aljazeera and Arabia news channels and would speculate about Israeli assault and Hamas defence plans. The thing about war though, was it fucked everyone's mind, and a lot of people followed the crowds blindly by following the news so closely. But deep down we were all scared.

'Well, I must say I have never heard anything like that, and it certainly impresses me that a couple can love each other so much that the whole thing outside doesn't matter to them. It's the sort of thing I've only seen in movies, but little did I know it was here on my doorstep in Gaza City. *Mashi*, okay, if that's the case, well, why did he go out the night of the 19th July 2014 – the night he was killed – while a massacre was going on? And before you say that he didn't know it was happening, because he didn't listen to the news, he must have figured it out. The bombing could be heard from far away. People were talking about it all over Gaza, so someone on the street must have told him. What did he tell you exactly?'

'He said he needed a break from our routine. He had received a text that his friends were meeting in El Saha and decided to go and join them. I was happy for him to go, as I was worried he was getting depressed. I thought a good outing with old mates would do him good–'

'Who are the friends?' Nouman interrupted.

'Hmm . . . not sure,' I answered hesitantly.

'Concentrate, please – give me names?'

'He didn't say, honestly. I am not trying to hide it.'

'And you didn't ask?' Nouman's voice was softening.

'No.' Yet again, I somehow started crying. Was I offended, angry?

'I am sorry Mrs. Tanani, we can stop here if you like. I can only imagine how difficult it must be for you. Let me get you a cup of coffee.'

'No thanks.'

'Water?'

'Yes please.' I looked away.

He pressed a button, and a young boy, who could barely have been thirteen years old, entered the office. Nouman placed the order and the boy returned in a flash to give me the bottle. He was beautiful, with wide green eyes and very dark skin. His face was scarred a little and he was incredibly thin. He had that striking look which could surely put him on the cover of the *National Geographic* or an Oxfam charity poster.

'He lost all his family in the war.'

I nodded, not knowing what to say – that very same war that I ignored, that very same war that we pretended wasn't there. I wondered whether this thin human being had the same attitude to war, ignoring it and living his life just like any boy of his age would. Then, bang – the people around him disappeared. Or did he live it all? Was he aware it was a war we were going through? Did he hold on to his mother as death crept in and snatched her from him? Maybe death even looked back at him and laughed loudly. I wondered which one was easier, mine or his? To ignore death or wait for it to laugh in your face?

War . . . bloody war . . . it was everywhere and it never went away. We lived with it, and somehow it became familiar, the same way summer was to Gaza, or the scent of jasmine. If you had common sense, you could almost anticipate the date of the next war; normally after hopes had been raised high enough so people would think *khalas* – there would be no more wars. Then it would hit, just like a car crash. Our first reaction would be 'Holy shit, I am still alive'. Then we would start expecting and mourning the damage.

'Did you try to call him when you heard of the massacre?'

'I didn't know there was a massacre; I carried on with the same routine.'

Nouman was rolling his eyes now; he clearly wasn't convinced.

'I promise you, I didn't.'

'*Mashi*, at what time did you finally call him?'

'2 a.m. on the morning of the 20th July.'

'His phone was off I am assuming.'

'Yes.'

'What did you do afterwards?'

'Nothing – I lay in bed and waited. I tried again half an hour later, and still the phone was off. I tried once more, an hour later, and then I fell asleep – I was exhausted. At 9:30 a.m. there was still no sign of him. I went out on the balcony to see if he was there or if he was on the street. There was nothing; no one was on the street. I scrolled through my phone trying to find the names of any of Ammar's friends. I called a few numbers; some did not answer and others just said they didn't know his whereabouts and that they had not seen him for a long time. Only Sameeh, his friend from university, who now worked at the municipality, asked questions about the situation and why he had suddenly received a phone call from his friend's wife. I explained what had happened and he asked if I needed any help.'

Recounting those memories, I could feel a lump forming in my throat, blocking the words from coming out, and when they did emerge they were stuck, bubbling on the surface of my tongue.

Nouman was silent: he watched me; he understood; he poured some water into a clear glass and walked over to hand it to me. I drank it while looking at him, towering above me. I was afraid, though of what I wasn't sure. I felt fragile.

'Would you like to stop, Mrs. Tanani? I am happy for us to carry on tomorrow.'

'No,' I said hastily, 'I would like to continue if it's okay.'

'Yes, of course.'

'It was Sameeh who told me the news, around 4 p.m. the day after I phoned everyone. He called my mobile and told me he had heard Ammar's name on the news. For some reason he expected me to know. My two brothers were sitting on the sofa in the front room when I screamed. They had come to visit me as Mother wasn't feeling well and had sent them to be with me instead. The massacre was coming to an end then. Issa and Jamil had the news blasting out in the living room, which gave a minute-by-minute update of what was happening. They ran to the bedroom where I was lying on the floor, the broken Nokia phone handset beside me where I had I dropped it after I received the news.

'Jamil started shouting,'*Ya Allah*, what happened to you?' Issa held me up, put my hand on his shoulder and walked me back to the living room. 'We have a crazy sister,' I heard Jamil tell him, as Issa walked to the kitchen to get a glass of water. As they came back into the room, the name Ammar Bseiso was being read out on TV as one of the one hundred and twenty people killed on that fateful night.

'"*La Hawla Wala Qwoata Illa Billah* – no solution or power except with God." Jamil and Issa said it together at exactly the same time. I can hardly remember anything after that. I just found myself in the family house in Jabalia Camp a few hours later, lying in Mother's bed. She was praying as I opened my eyes, dressed in her white prayer clothes. She looked at me as she finished, and came close, while taking off her headscarf. '*Taqabal Allah Mama* – God accept your prayers, Mum,' I said as she started to tell me how strong I should be and that Ammar was a martyr waiting for me in heaven. To tell you the truth, I didn't want her to tell me any of that, because I knew Ammar didn't believe in it. I wanted her to stop; the more she continued, the lonelier I felt.'

'I am sorry,' Nouman said, suddenly. 'I feel for you, I can understand it must have been very difficult to cope with both things at the same time – your loss and alienation.'

No one had ever said that to me in my entire life; nobody understood, no one even attempted to understand, let alone offer a solution. Two simple words, loss and alienation, summed up exactly how I felt that day. I thought afterwards that I couldn't have described it any more concisely or sympathetically than that. I looked at him for a long time. I cried again and he brought a tissue over. He never took his eyes off me. A lot of people saw me cry while roaming

Gaza looking for a detective, but they always looked away and passed by me as if I didn't exist.

'Let me take a step back if you don't mind,' Nouman said 'Why Sameeh? And who is he?'

'I don't know; I told you, he was the only one who answered my phone calls. He was one of Ammar's university friends.'

'And you didn't keep in touch? I mean you don't seem to know him well.'

'Yes – we stayed in touch and met frequently.' I responded with certainty.

'And he was the first one to tell you the news?'

'Yes . . . why is this important?' I asked sharply.

'I am just trying to understand everything Mrs. Tanani. All details are important at this stage.'

There was something both frightening and reassuring about the tone of his voice – scary in the sense that I did not know how police investigations worked, I never trusted the police in the first instance. The way they asked leading questions was unsettling – it gave me the feeling of being interrogated, of being put on the spot. Yet the way Nouman spoke gave the reassurance that he was in charge, that he knew what he was doing and all I needed to do was trust him and believe he would get a grip on everything.

'I think we should stop now; we can continue tomorrow if you are free.'

'I am free,' I said.

'Very well, *inshallah* we will continue talking tomorrow. Please be here at 9 a.m. sharp.' He closed his notebook.

'I want a list of names of everyone – friends, enemies, neighbours, cousins, third cousins, the whole lot. I want to know how they all knew Ammar.'

'Of course. You will have that. Thank you for listening to my story. It's been a while. My brothers and Mother have heard enough of it now.'

He nodded, stood up and put out his hand to shake mine.

'Are you okay now? How are you feeling?' His hand was stretching towards me.

'I feel like I've just had a caesarean.'

'How do you know how that feels, you have never had a baby let alone a C-section?'

We both laughed, knowing that the joke was bad, but that was the only thing we could do.

Chapter 5

Shortly after leaving the police station, I had the feeling I was being followed. The streets were busy. It had been a warm December day, one of those when the winter sun was so strong it felt as though spring had arrived early. The Mediterranean could have plenty of days like these in winter, a welcome break for people to warm their bodies after struggling in the damp of their unheated and uninsulated houses. There were a few puddles still here and there; the bottom of the *jilbab* I was wearing was already dirty, but the street smelled nice and earthy, and the side where the sun shone was already drying out.

Despite the distraction of the crowds on the street: bringing chairs outside so they could soak up the sun; kids playing with a half-deflated ball with a peeled off skin, I could feel the eyes of the person watching me. But every time I turned around, the street looked normal.

The whole thing started to feel like a horror film. In my mind, everyone there was following me; it felt as though they were creeping behind me, echoing my footsteps, and when my head turned they would stop and pretend to go back to their normal activity. Without much forethought, I started running, noises crashing around me. Someone was laughing loudly, another was smoking his *shisha*, but blowing massive clouds of smoke.

I kept running in the opposite direction to my house, up towards the El Ansar Complex where the British stationed themselves during World War One. My body was heating up, but I kept running faster and faster. Then . . . blackness. I fell. I hit something, or did something hit me?

At El Shifa hospital, the young doctor gave me a small

plastic bag full of painkillers and told me to go to my local medical practice to change my bandages after three days.

'You are lucky the cut wasn't deeper than this,' he said as he signed some papers.

'How did it happen, doctor?'

'You hit something,' he said matter-of-factly, without even looking at me. 'You were running and you must not have seen the lamp post ahead of you.'

'But the cut is in my back? How could I have hit myself in the back?' He stopped fiddling with his papers and looked at me fiercely, as if I had offended his pride somehow.

'How the hell am I supposed to know? I wasn't there was I?' He stood up, ushering me outside while fishing in his pockets for his mobile phone. 'You could've fallen on the kerb,' he murmured.

'Doctor, was it a kerb or a lamp post? I am genuinely trying to understand what happened and not doubting your expertise.' This seemed to calm him a little. He sighed and told me he wasn't sure, and that given the shortage of staff at the hospital he didn't have time to investigate further.

When I walked outside, I felt so dizzy I had to take a private cab all the way back home. Was I losing it? Not now, please – not after finally finding my detective. What would Nouman say when I told him? Would he believe anything after this? I decided I'd better keep it quiet. It was just a minor incident anyway, he didn't need to know.

Who was following me and why? What did they want from me? The thought of being alone in the flat frightened me. What if someone turned up and tried to murder me? Well, that would certainly be a solution to my troubles. I had thought about suicide many times. The thought of ending all this misery crossed my mind a thousand times over, it kept me awake at night, it frightened me and in some strange way also gave me hope. The idea kept me going, offering a final resolution after I had found the detective who would take my case, after justice had prevailed, after my brothers were proven wrong and so on and so forth. But it was strange that the feeling of taking my own life was far less scary than someone else doing the job for me.

I needed safety that night and there was nowhere for me to go except back home to Jabalia Camp. The trade-off was that I had to listen to hours of boring conversations between my sisters-in-law and receive a few dirty looks from Jamil.

My mother didn't normally cook anything special on a Tuesday; she would probably be doing the washing this evening. I could help her and do some housework there. I would do anything mundane to take my mind off things; my only concern was how to explain to Jamil and Issa what had happened to my back.

I got there around 4 p.m. and, to my shock, there was no one at home. This never happened; there was always someone there. The kids would be returning from school any minute after their afternoon classes in the nearby Madaris Street. The front door was open. Without thinking, I rushed inside and called for Mother and my two brothers, but none of them were there. I went to their bedrooms, to the kitchen, to the bathroom, up the stairs onto the roof, and just as I was about to shout out for our nosy neighbour, Um Salah, and ask her what had happened, I heard Jamil downstairs roaring with anger.

'Why the hell didn't you let me run after him?' He was shouting at Mother, hovering near her as though he wanted to push her out of his way.

'What good would it have done my son? He is out now, he is not here and we are all safe.'

'Mother, what happened? Where were you guys?' I ran down the stairs, much to my family's astonishment. They looked shocked to see me, unsure how to react.

'Are you all alright? When I came in the house was empty and the front door was open. What happened?'

'That's all I need right now, another one asking questions,' Jamil muttered under his breath.

'Someone tried to break into the house and Jamil went out chasing him. We all followed him in case he did permanent damage to the poor soul.'

Mother was looking at me with big wide eyes, as if telling me to come down and give her a hug. There was something about this woman that brought calmness to the chaos around her. She was in control and she knew it – no matter what noise people made around her, no matter how angry or frightened everyone was, she knew what to say and how to reassure everyone. I started to go down the stairs, was relieved to embrace her to avoid Jamil's angry looks.

'He was saying something as he ran away,' said Jamil's wife, Basma.

'Yes, he was shouting "Tell her to stop!"' Issa's wife replied.

Jamil was furious with both of them; he was shouting at the top of his voice, telling them to shut up. Then he turned around to me. 'It's all your fault,' he blurted.

A tear fell as I hugged Mother tightly, and she patted my shoulders gently as if to say 'there, there'. It was what I needed; nothing else could have been better right then.

Not only had I been knocked out by some stranger following me in the street, but now my brother was accusing me of disturbing the harmony in his life – as if that life was happy and peaceful in the first place.

Jamil hadn't always been angry as a kid; nobody understood how it happened. But I thought he had turned more aggressive after Father died. He was a peaceful, beautiful child, but when Father got cancer, we couldn't find the right medication for him in Gaza so we needed to get him to Israel for medical treatment. The Israeli authorities refused to grant him admittance on the grounds of security. 'What security?' raged ten-year-old Jamil. Like many Palestinian farmers who were kicked out of their villages by Israel in 1948, Father had turned to construction to earn a living. He made his way up the ranks very quickly and became a major contractor in Israel, building most of Tel Aviv. He used to bring Palestinian workers to Israel in the 80s and 90s to undertake construction work. Father always travelled freely in and out of Gaza through the Erez Crossing, so why not when he needed the medication? Jamil couldn't understand that at all, he was furious. Palestinian Authority officials applied to the Israelis on our behalf for a permit but it was never granted. Being from Gaza killed him eventually.

After that, Jamil turned into an angry child: picking fights with older kids on the street; throwing people's bins into the middle of the road; assaulting older men for no apparent reason. Poor Issa had to assume the father's role quickly while having to deal with a disturbed younger brother. The embarrassment during the funeral, when Jamil threw all the bitter coffee on the floor and refused to serve anyone, was the first test for Issa to assert his authority as the new male figure in the family. I saw a tear in Issa's eye as he pushed his younger brother inside the house and beat him up in one of the rooms. I heard Jamil groaning with pain and wanted to go inside and help him, to tell Issa to stop, but I never did. Maybe this is why Jamil hated me so much.

Chapter 6

That evening, I lay in bed and tried to remember everything – going through all the names of people we both knew. I tried to remember the last few days of Ammar's life, wracking my brain to see if he had called anyone during our voluntary house arrest. He spoke to his mother, and he once phoned the neighbour, Abu Mohammed, because he couldn't be bothered to go downstairs. I wasn't sure how far back Nouman wanted me to go, and I started to recall the first time we met, at the beginning of autumn in 1999.

It was during the first year at El Azhar University, when our professor, who was teaching us Shakespeare at the time, decided the best way for us to understand the literary genius of the man was to enact *Richard II*.

Ammar was the obvious candidate for the star role. His fair skin, his gentleness, and his ability to speak fluent English with hardly any accent, made the casting very easy. Had he been auditioning for the part of Othello, it would have been a completely different story, but *Richard II*, the gentle-yet-twisted king, was no problem at all. Little did I know that they also had something else in common – dying young.

I, on the other hand, struggled to obtain a role, but was eventually offered the part of the 4th Countess of Kent; wife to Edward the Black Prince and mother to none other than Richard himself. When my classmate, Hana, turned down the role because her conservative father refused to allow her to act alongside men, our dear professor struggled to find a replacement and had to settle for me. He didn't think I was good acting material.

'Acting is not for refugees from the Jabalia Camp,' he once said, as he brushed me aside. But now, he came begging for me to take the role. I said I would think about it, and left him hanging for three whole days before I officially accepted the role. That was my revenge for his snobbery. But deep down I wanted the role so much, it was something new to try, something I had never done.

I felt sorry for Hana, but was pleased to be able to take the part. Of course, I didn't tell my family what I was doing. Professor Othman wanted us to perform at the graduation ceremonies the following year, but we still had to have intensive rehearsals, staying late sometimes. This was our first shot at a possible acting career, which we knew from the outset was a very remote prospect. Still, it was a once-in-a-lifetime opportunity. It was part of our escape; a window that gave us a glimpse of what life could have been like had we been born in London, or anywhere peaceful for that matter. Eventually, I told Mother what I was doing, and she told my siblings I was spending time in the library. Ammar and I spent a lot of time together rehearsing with the rest of the cast, and our professor, who thought he was the best director in the whole of the Gaza Strip. One day, Ammar asked me if I could stay later to rehearse a couple of lines together.

> *Let us sit upon the ground*
> *And tell sad stories of the death of kings;*
> *How some have been deposed; some slain in war,*
> *Some haunted by the ghosts they have deposed;*
> *Some poison'd by their wives: some sleeping kill'd;*
> *All murder'd: for within the hollow crown*
> *That rounds the mortal temples of a king*
> *Keeps Death his court and there the antic sits,*
> *Scoffing his state and grinning at his pomp,*
> *Allowing him a breath…*

I was breathless. I had never heard anything like this before. I had read the script of course, but for some reason, this particular speech hadn't registered with me. It was always difficult to decode the Old English Shakespeare used, especially when we were just reading it. Although we were a few weeks into rehearsals then, I hadn't had the chance to hear this speech before. We had been focussing on the big scenes with the other actors. Professor Othman wanted us to work on our own to perfect our individual speeches, thus using the limited rehearsal time to focus on the battle scene, the deposing of the king, Gloucester arriving at the palace. He also wanted us to practice the final scene of dethroning the old king and placing the wonky cardboard, glitter-filled crown on the new king.

We stayed in the classroom for hours until security came to kick us out; questioning what we were doing and whether we were up to something improper. I could listen to Ammar speaking for the whole evening and for some reason he made me very sympathetic towards the stupid king. I wasn't sure whether Shakespeare wanted us to feel that way or not. But I didn't care; I had found my king whom I admired enormously and who would have my allegiance forever. I called him 'your majesty' for years after that and it always made him smile – he was very fond of that role.

The final performance in July 2000 took place in the main square outside the university, which was normally used as a bus station. There was a large crowd of people from both our year and the rest of the university. We had an audience of over five thousand people, and after the long, boring speech given by the president about what he described as a 'great institution', the nerves kicked in. I had that crunching feeling in my stomach and all I wanted to do was run away. Ammar held my hands in the makeshift dressing room beneath the massive stage, which was being cleared for our performance. I could hear stomping and sound checks taking place right above us. At that moment, I felt that he wanted me to be there – my Ammar didn't want me to run away.

'Let's do this together,' he said, and smiled. I nervously lowered my head and let him touch my hair quickly before the rest of the cast noticed.

The performance took place at 2 p.m. in the scorching heat of the July sun. I searched through the audience and saw many familiar faces, and to my surprise I saw Mother standing there, completely engrossed in the performance. Although she didn't speak any English, like most people in the audience she was following everything, focussing on each character and what they did on stage. It made me smile to think of this great woman who had come all the way from Jabalia Camp to the big city to be with her daughter, without even understanding a word. She clapped so hard when we bowed to the audience, then she turned back and disappeared into the crowd. And as if it was some sort of national festival, jets flew overhead just as the audience applauded. People began to panic, as this was a signal that the Israelis were about to bomb somewhere. There were a couple of police stations nearby which always took the hits of the Israeli attacks, even when they were completely empty.

People started to run, causing a stampede. We could hear the sound of sirens in the distance. In ten minutes, the whole square was empty save for a few students who were unfazed by the situation, along with Ammar and I. We decided to take a walk to the beach past the museum of Palestinian crafts and El Ansar Complex.

We turned left alongside Yasser Arafat's compound and walked along the road towards Abu Mazen roundabout, then right towards El Shalihat Beach Club, where we found a table and ordered a *shisha* and fruit cocktails. Lionel Richie was playing in the background; 'Hello' was mixing with the sound of waves and children playing. We looked at each other and I knew we were in love; two people from totally different worlds now found themselves on a beach in Gaza, listening to Western music and playing Shakespeare. For some reason,

Lionel Richie was very famous in Gaza and across Palestine. People loved him and played his songs over and over.

After that day, we became inseparable. We had shared Shakespeare and sat beneath Israeli bombs with the beautiful lyrics of 'Hello' ringing louder in our ears than anything else. I knew it was Ammar I was looking for and that the feeling was mutual. It was a bond difficult to break. Or so I thought at the time.

**

After my second date with Ammar, he introduced me to his friend Sameeh who was studying Business and Commerce at Al Azhar University. Sameeh joined us during many of our early dates. I wasn't overly impressed at first, but Ammar said they were like brothers and didn't hide anything from each other.

Sameeh was extremely kind to me. We talked about Ammar a lot, and whenever we had an argument he would be there to listen to me. It was great to have a male figure to talk to who understood, someone I could discuss the relationship with – as family or neighbours would have simply called me a whore. And when Jamil banned me from seeing Ammar, it was Sameeh who insisted that we should continue to meet each other and said he would be happy to provide any cover if needed.

That cover was very much appreciated. I often asked Sameeh to phone the family home and pretend he was our course administrator. He would phone and say that the last class of the day, 'Dickens: Profiting from Social Injustice in Nineteenth Century England', was running late and that students were required to stay a couple of hours beyond the normal end time of 4 p.m. Sameeh took a while to learn the long title, which he would say very quickly over the phone whenever he spoke to my family. His face would be pale immediately afterwards, especially if it was Jamil on the other end. Poor Sameeh wouldn't speak for a few minutes afterwards, and all he could come up with was, 'Well, that was close'.

We normally went to the café in the Consulat General de France on Charles de Gaulle Street, just a few hundred metres down the hill from Al Azhar University. Ammar liked the outdoor café, which once even offered alcohol. But he never liked the people there, he always called them "culturally colonised people".

"You see, people who learn English do so because it is functional – they may want to travel, trade, communicate . . . etcetera. But those learning French do so because they want to look superior." He would say those exact words almost every time we went there.

'I am not sure about that,' I'd answer, 'I think French can be functional too. It's like any language I suppose, but I like the fact that English is not the only language in the world.'

Ammar was never convinced by my argument, but we didn't prolong these discussions, so as not to waste the precious time we had together.

Sameeh would sit on a separate table and read the *Al Ayyam* Palestinian newspaper, doing the crossword. He looked completely out of place there with everyone around looking affluent and reading big books in French. He also felt uncomfortable with the way he dressed. Unlike Ammar, Sameeh was a typical Palestinian guy, wearing heavy jeans in the heat of summer. He had thick hair and a beard which made him look much older. He was tall and muscular with piercing black eyes which made him seem very intense.

They were very close friends. Ammar would always check things with him before doing anything, almost as if he was seeking Sameeh's approval – even when we held hands across the table. Ammar would glance towards Sameeh first before looking me in the eyes. It annoyed me whenever he did this, so I had to ask him to stop and questioned why he'd been doing it in the first place. But he never gave a good explanation.

Of course, there were a few other friends around; those whom Ammar knew from his neighbourhood and were studying other subjects. But he never introduced me to any of them. Our eyes would glance across the tables in the small Jawaharlal Nehru University Library, which had been donated to us by the government of India.

We would smile as Ammar did his best to hide the situation from his friends. Occasionally, they would look across at me, confused.

As soon as he finished with them, he would walk across to my table and ask me to go for lunch. And Sameeh always joined us too. After we got married, we continued to see Sameeh regularly. He practically lived in our house. He was always the quiet type, so it was never a problem having him around. I would just retreat to my bedroom and leave the two friends drinking coffee and catching up in the living room as they watched TV and listened to the news.

Ammar's friend became my newly adopted brother, given that my own siblings didn't care much about me. I was too removed from Issa in his fatherly position, and Jamil was the crazy one who hated me and Ammar. Sameeh and I became very close. He would even come over when my husband wasn't at home and make himself comfortable in the living room. Of course, this was unheard of in Gaza; people would go mad if they knew a single guy and a married woman were on their own in a flat. But Ammar never minded coming home late and finding his friend waiting for him. In fact, on the very few days that Sameeh wasn't there, my husband would ask after him. He would then text or phone him to check that he was okay.

But we lost touch with Sameeh in the last year before Ammar's death. He just stopped coming to visit us. Ammar didn't want to talk about it, so I assumed they had fallen out for some reason and didn't want to press the issue. I didn't see him at all – except for once. I was walking down the Gold Market in El Saha, rushing to grab a cab to Jabalia Camp to visit my family. When I got in the taxi, there they were, Ammar and Sameeh, having a *shawarma* sandwich at Abu El Abed restaurant in El Saha. I tried to shout hello to both of them but they didn't hear me, and the driver hurried off, having filled the car with two other men next to me in the back, and a woman and her two small children in the front passenger seat. I was happy to see the two old friends reunited again. They looked like they were having a great time.

When I got home that evening, I was surprised that Ammar did not mention it. He talked mainly about his day at work, translating official documents at the UN office where he worked. Not wanting to look like a controlling wife, I decided not to ask and just left him to it.

***

I too lost touch with most of my friends after we got married, except for my beautiful friend Wafa, who was from Khan Younis. We met in the second year at university, when the Second Intifada kicked off. The Israelis started to install 'flying checkpoints' – cutting off the main roads between north and south Gaza. So she often stayed with me in Jabalia Camp. It was nice to have female company in the house who wasn't family and didn't have all the baggage my sisters-in-law did. We talked for hours at night, studied together and gossiped a lot about Ammar and boys in our year. At home, we spoke in English, so no one could understand. She had a perfect American accent, which she said had been acquired by watching endless episodes of the soap opera, *Beauty and the Beast* – the finest American TV crap.

She was beautiful, with very deep olive skin and wide

brown eyes. Ammar didn't like her much for some reason. He said she was too conservative for him; although the only signs of this she ever showed were the long black *jilbab* and white headscarf she wore.

She was a tall woman, who attracted the attention of lustful men wherever she went. She was such an honest person who always spoke her mind, no matter what the consequences were. This sometimes got her into trouble and perhaps was the reason Ammar did not get on well with her. They argued a lot and it made me laugh whenever she told him that he was politically naïve.

After we got married, Ammar avoided her completely, and whenever he got home and found her there he would make an excuse and leave immediately. It annoyed me considerably that he behaved that way towards my friend. I tried to talk to him about it, but it just made it worse, so I decided to accept it.

Eventually, we started meeting almost in secret. Well, it wasn't really that way, but I didn't feel as though I had to tell him when I was meeting her, and he never asked. There were the occasional awkward moments when he asked what I had done on a certain day and I had to avoid mentioning Wafa.

She found my husband strange and deluded and once said that he was "trapped inside his own mind". I didn't know what that meant and therefore didn't really take any notice of it. A lot of people found Ammar's dreamy self a little bit weird. It was too much juxtaposed against the harsh reality of Gaza. But that was the very same thing which made me fall madly in love with him – his indifference to the world around him.

Wafa and Sameeh became good friends too, given that they both spent a lot of time together in my flat. Wafa would often come and find Sameeh sitting on the sofa, smoking and drinking coffee.

"Don't you have a home to go to?" she would ask him as

he looked at her in complete bewilderment, as if to say "what business do you have to ask"? But slowly they got to know each other and eventually they got on well. We played endless *tarneeb* card games together when Ammar came home, and ate, smoked and listened to the news. Wafa also found it strange that Sameeh disappeared suddenly and stopped coming. She tried to contact him to find out what had happened, but she told me that he never answered her calls.

When I became a widow in July 2014, Wafa was there for me all the time. She went out a few times to try and discover the truth about what had happened to Ammar, and helped me spread the word on Facebook and Twitter. But by then, she had three kids and a very demanding husband who did not respect her job as a freelance editor for a new English language media outlet. After a year of looking and not finding any clues, her energy to help me dwindled, while I continued to go crazy. Everybody called me a mad woman; Jamil even called the Gaza Community Mental Health Programme and scheduled a meeting for me, which of course I refused to attend.

So our handsome foursome broke up completely – first, we became three when Sameeh abandoned our gatherings, then two when my husband was killed and finally one when everyone around me disappeared. Not many people understood this loss, what it felt like to lose the person who was there next to you all the time. What it meant to be alone. People thought the pain of losing someone was about what was going on at that point in time, about missing their company, but it wasn't for me. It was about the lack of a future, the fact that I had to go through life by myself. And the idea of organising my life on my own without considering my man, my king, his majesty, was suffocating me. It made me panic, and I woke up shouting in the middle of the night. It made me want to end all this misery.

'Who killed my husband?' was the question I went to bed with and woke up with. 'Who took him away?' It was driving me crazy.

Chapter 7

'Alright, Mrs. Tanani.'

'Zahra, please,' I gently reminded Nouman. He was sitting behind the same desk, clicking the down arrow on his white keyboard, while staring at the screen. There was something about his intense look that was very intriguing. I was tempted to go and look over his shoulder to see what he was staring at. Was it related to my case or was he simply reading the news?

'I need you to tell me about the people you saw during the war period only. We will expand the timeline a little later, but let's focus on this for now shall we?'

'You are wearing glasses,' I said excitedly, having just noticed as I took the seat opposite his desk.

'Yes, for reading and computer screens only. You need these things when you get to my age.'

'Twenty-five?' My mouth spread into a wide open smile and his eyes gleamed at me. There was so much kindness in those eyes, the type I had almost forgotten.

'Yes, that's right. Twenty-five; it is all in the heart as they say. Now, give me all the names please.'

'Well I told you, there weren't many. We locked ourselves up, hiding away from it all, pretending it wasn't happening. We saw some neighbours, Abu Mohmmed was always on the street smoking and watching the jets in the sky. Um Shihada, our nosy neighbour, knocked on our door a few times to check that our families were fine. We stayed on the balcony and chatted to a few people here and there as they passed by on the street or came home from work. It was such a stressful time for everyone; they all looked like they had just escaped from a zombie film.'

'So, no friends at all?'

'No. Our only friends were Sameeh and Wafa. We stopped seeing Ammar's friend a year earlier when they fell out, and Wafa became busy with her husband, Mahmoud, and her kids.'

'Why did they fall out?' Nouman was now typing.

'I am not sure, Ammar never said.'

'And you didn't ask?' he said sarcastically.

'No, I didn't want to get involved between the two friends. I realised that Ammar was upset about it, so I thought not to add insult to injury by asking too many questions.'

'Okay, what about relatives?' Nouman asked, frustrated.

'No, we spoke to them by phone only.'

'And your two brothers and mother never came to visit you?'

'No, because they were afraid. Everywhere was dangerous; no one wanted to leave their families alone, especially young children. They were all frightened. Jamil disappeared for some time. He always did that whenever there was a war on Gaza. Issa was the only man in the house and Mother begged him not to go anywhere – she didn't want him out of her sight. Besides, everyone in Gaza thought the whole war would be over soon, a week or two maximum. No one expected it to last for fifty-one days!'

'I see,' said Nouman. He stopped scrolling down on his keyboard, took his glasses off, put both elbows on the desk and leant forward.

'You see, that's what I am finding difficult to comprehend, Zahra. You locked yourself up for a while, and in any case you didn't have much of a social life after getting married, but somehow, on a night when a massacre was happening, your husband decided to go and have *shisha* with some friends. And you didn't think to ask who these friends were or where they suddenly appeared from?!'

'Er . . . no, I did not. I told you I was glad to see him

going out. I was worried he was becoming depressed.'

'So, no one for almost twenty days up to that night. Can you confirm that?'

'Hmm . . . no, wait there was one time when Ammar left the house for a while. A week or ten days after the war had started.'

'A week or ten days? Which is it, Zahra?'

'I don't know, I am trying to remember.' My brain was spinning; the trouble with the damn war was that it made the days melt into each other; days were as dark as long nights, weekdays phased into weekends in one continuous wait, expecting death to put an end to it all. Somehow, I lived in the past rather than the present to avoid going crazy.

'Okay, where did he go?' Nouman interrupted my thoughts.

'There was a woman . . . yes . . . she came to our flat.'

'A woman?'

'Yes, a blonde one, she was foreign . . . she spoke English. She wasn't wearing a headscarf, had a tight green top and black jeans. Yes, I remember this because I was surprised to find her on our doorstep. Ammar came and introduced her as Celine. He said she needed some translation doing for her report. She sat on the sofa as Ammar went to the bathroom and got ready. She was awfully polite and asked a lot of questions about the situation and what we were doing to keep safe. She asked after my family and said that she was a freelance journalist preparing a short report to send to foreign media. I asked Ammar how it went when he came back later and he said it was hard to get people to talk, they were distressed, and that he saw some nasty stuff, destroyed buildings with people still in them. He wanted us to go back to our lock up in the bedroom and forget about the whole thing.'

Nouman was staring at me so hard, a couple of drops of sweat appeared on his forehead. He was silent, wanting me to carry on. But I didn't have much to add.

'I think she was French.'

'How do you know that?' Asked Nouman quickly.

'Well, she spoke English with a foreign accent. I studied English Literature and did phonetics. We had to listen to endless tapes of different accents from around the world. The French one fascinated me. Besides, the name would indicate that. I read that somewhere. There was a novel we had to write an essay about, I can't remember which one, but anyway the heroine, Celine, was French.'

Nouman got his notebook out from the top drawer of his desk and wrote down everything I said. His eyes were getting smaller the more he focussed on me.

'How long did they spend outside?'

'I don't know . . . four hours . . . or maybe six?'

'A woman came and took your husband away for more than four hours and you did not think to ask more questions? Zahra, what's wrong with you?'

'Nothing is wrong,' I replied sharply, offended by the suggestion that I was a careless wife.

'We never asked questions; we just trusted each other. Ammar always said he wanted to be different from other couples in Gaza, that he wanted us to be a 'modern' couple.'

'Okay, so was it a week or ten days after the war started?'

'Wait, the war started on the 6th July, right? Yes, that's right . . . it must have been ten days after then . . . I remember now because Ammar said that the war wouldn't last more than two weeks and we had already entered the second one then. He reckoned we had four days left.'

'How did he come to this conclusion?'

'I don't know. Everyone in Gaza always has a political theory, don't you?'

'I tend to avoid that,' said Nouman, looking back at his screen. 'This is an unusual place, Zahra, anything could happen here . . . I learned not to theorise so that I don't get more frustrated than I already am.' He clicked the mouse twice. 'I am looking at last year's calendar here, so ten days after the war started was the 16th July and you are saying Ammar was killed on the night of the Shujaia massacre which happened on the night of the 19th July, all the way through to the early hours of 20th July. That means Celine came to your place three days before your husband died.'

The revelation stunned me – I had completely forgotten this, and now faced with it, I felt my stomach turn. My face must have gone completely pale, as Nouman asked me if I wanted a glass of water. He got up and went out, and when he came back and handed it to me, I realised that I didn't flinch at all.

'Are you alright?' he asked, in a compassionate voice which brought me back to reality.

'Yes . . . yes . . . sorry.' I wiped my face with my hands.

'Okay, let's leave this for now. Tell me, did Ammar have any enemies? Someone who might wish him dead?'

'No,' I said sharply.

'You never saw him argue with anyone?'

'No!'

'Are you sure? It is hard to believe – that's what we do best in Gaza. We argue all the time. About the lack of water, about electricity, and we take it out on each other. This is what bloody occupation has done to us.' He was staring down at the Hamas logo on the headed paper on his desk.

'Ammar wasn't like that. He always let things go. Whenever an argument broke out with a neighbour, he would just walk away. He would say "Fine, have it your way", and just simply find a different method of getting what he wanted. I supposed that's why everyone liked him on the street.'

'What about you? Did you have any enemies?'

'Me? God, no . . . why? I am not dead . . . yet anyway.'

'I didn't mean it that way. Sometimes these things happen – people get their revenge by harming their enemy's family members or loved ones.'

'Do you have any enemies, Mr. Nouman?'

'If I can't call you Mrs. Zahra, then you can't call me Mr. Nouman,' he said with a big smile on his face, which made me uncomfortable. 'Well, I've caught a few criminals in my life, I must have enemies, of course. I'm sure I am not that well-liked in some circles, but that's fine. It's an occupational hazard I'm afraid.'

I wanted him to talk more, to tell me about his life, the whole thing. I knew virtually nothing about him. I was intrigued by this calm man who seemed to focus mainly on his career. In a way he was a little like Ammar, living in a different world; Ammar's was dreamy and Nouman's was practical, with a mission to catch criminals. The trouble with the two of them was that living in Gaza was so not like that. The reality of the occupation interfered with everything in everyone's lives, even their sex life sometimes. There was once a project sponsored by the UN to spread awareness of contraception. They spent thousands of dollars going around talking to communities, and when people finally learned about and trusted condoms, the bloody Israelis didn't allow them in. So lots more babies were born. Ammar joked that "it was good to have more babies, it was a demographic battle after all".

'Can I ask you a question?' Nouman stopped writing and looked at me.

'Of course.'

'Did you love your husband?'

The question stunned me, as if someone had pushed me into deep cold water. It was out of order for him to feel he could ask that, how dare he doubt my love for my husband?

I didn't answer, simply stood up and headed for the door.

'Tell me, when did you two last argue?' He spoke loudly, which made me stop.

'What, generally?'

'I am interested in the period up to Ammar's death. Of course, I am not after a record of your entire married life.'

I felt offended by this statement. Nouman had this ability of turning into a bureaucrat with just a few words.

'Well, we argued like all couples did – what to watch, who last did the washing up, who should answer the phone if it ever rang. Those sorts of things. At the beginning, I was angry with him for not going out to see his family during the war.'

'Did he ban you from seeing your family?' Nouman interrupted.

'No.'

'Fine, tell me about his parents. Where do they live, how can I get in touch?'

'Ammar has a big extended family. You know the Bseisos. You are from Gaza City so you must know the family.'

'Yes I do, of course. Gazan families know each other well. The Bseisos have always boasted of their authentic relationship to this land. They like to believe they are the landlords of the entire Strip. But I don't know Ammar's parents. I don't believe I have ever met them.'

'They live near Tel El Hawwa, not very far from here. Just after the uni–'

'I know where that is,' Nouman interrupted.

'Both parents are architects. They run their own practice named after them, Salman and Rabab Practice. Well, they are retired now, but still take on a few projects.'

'Is there much designing happening in Gaza these days?' Nouman asked drily.

'Well, not if we can't get cement in, so they must be designing tents for refugees. I am sure there's a lot of business there.'

We both laughed out loud. His eyes were beaming, he looked very relaxed.

'Do you see them often?'

'Not very often, but yes, sometimes. His dad, Salman, calls in to check on me every now and again. But I never see Rabab. I never liked her anyway, so I am not dying over it.' He was still smiling, as if I was delivering some kind of stand-up comedy sketch.

'So Sameeh was the first person to break the news of Ammar's death to you? Did you see him after that?'

'No.'

Nouman removed his glasses and looked at me with something like pity in his eyes.

'Zahra, if I were to recite your answers to most of my questions you would probably think the person talking was mad. Someone, who used to be a good friend, phones you to tell you of your husband's death but you don't see him afterwards. I mean, did he come to the funeral?'

'There was hardly any funeral – you know lots of people were dying, the war was still raging. After burying the body on the same day, Ammar's parents decided to receive people's condolences in their apartment and didn't have a three-day wake for him as people normally do. So Sameeh never had the chance to come.'

'Did he try to phone again?'

'Yes, I saw a number of missed calls from him but I never called him back.'

How could a man understand what a woman felt like in the aftermath of her husband's death? It was difficult to explain to Nouman, to say to him that I did not want to speak to anyone or hear a man's voice again. I wondered whether men felt the same if they lost their wives or girlfriends. In Gaza, men would marry very quickly after their wives passed away, whether through an Israeli attack or nature taking its course. It would take women a long time to remarry though; no one would be interested in them unless a married man came along with ten children and wanted a second wife to help with the housework, while the first matriarchal wife sat in the middle of the house and did fuck all. I did not want to be that person, which was why I refused all the marriage proposals Jamil passed on to me through Mother and Issa.

But still, I should have talked to Sameeh. After all, he was like a brother to me at some point. I wished we had had the chance to meet afterwards and talk through everything, including why he fell out with his best friend and why we hadn't seen him for almost a year.

'Okay,' Nouman said, as he started to tidy up his desk, 'please write his number down, I would like to get in touch to ask him a few questions, but for now, I am afraid we are going to stop here. I need to be somewhere in half an hour. Please write your in-laws' phone number here as well.' He looked away as he handed me the piece of paper.

'When are we meeting next?'

'I am not sure,' he said, surprising me. 'I will get in touch.'

'Am I a suspect now?' I asked with fear in my eyes.

I felt sad to hear this, not to have a date to look forward to. For the first time, I felt powerless, as if I had no control over my story, having given it away. Worst of all was the fact that the man I fancied was now suspecting me.

Chapter 8

I was shocked to find Wafa waiting for me at the bottom of the stairs when I got home. Her face looked pale, melting into the shadow of the dark entrance of our building. She seemed tired.

'Mahmoud and I had a big argument. Can I stay with you for a few days? I don't want to go to my parents' place. They will ask a lot of questions which I can't face right now.'

She looked at me, pleading with me to accept, as if her life depended on it. I didn't know if I wanted her to stay or not. We hadn't seen each other for a long time and I had too much on my mind to be hospitable. But I just hugged her and led her upstairs. The apartment was cold and there was no electricity to switch on the mini electric heater Ammar bought from Fras Market. I closed the windows and left Wafa in the living room. When I came back, carrying a tray with two cups of Arabic coffee on it and a glass of water, Wafa put her phone away and smiled.

'I found a detective,' I said quickly. 'He has taken on the case and is currently investigating.'

Wafa got up and hugged me tightly, shouting with joy too close to my ear.

'Is he handsome?'

'Yes,' I replied without a moment's thought, realising how much I missed our catch-ups and gossip about men.

'How many children will you have to serve if you become the second wife?' she laughed as she started to guess the number on her fingers.

'None, actually.'

'What age is he, sixteen? All men are married in Gaza. That's our national entertainment, weddings. They are useless anyway, you marry someone and suddenly you become a slave not only to him, but to his family too. It is strange that your detective is not married and doesn't have any children. Did you ask him why?'

'No, it is not my place.'

'What do you mean it is not your place? That's what we do around here, we stick our nose into everything,' Wafa said matter-of-factly. 'How do you know that he is not married then?'

'I just guessed.'

'Has he caught the bastard then?'

'Well, we are only starting, you know. It is not a very easy case. Besides, the murder happened two years and five months ago. It will probably take some time before coming up with any theories.'

'Do you have a theory?' Wafa asked abruptly.

'Well, no, apart from the fact that he was murdered. But I have no way of knowing who, how and why? I have thought about it a million times, but now Nouman is asking questions about the details I feel like there is a lot of stuff to dig into.'

'What details?' Wafa asked.

'You should drink your coffee, it is getting cold. I need to go out for some shopping. Mother is coming tonight for dinner. She will be angry if she finds out that I didn't cook because I spent the day with a detective. Will you come with me?'

She put her headscarf on and long *jilbab*, sipped the last of her coffee and returned it to the tray. She was beaming with energy.

We walked down to El Saha, to the big Omari Mosque, to buy some supplies from the vegetable and meat market. I wanted to get some chicken to make Mother *musakhan*, her favourite dish. On the way, Wafa told me that her husband, Mahmoud, had become a lot more conservative than he used to be, and that he now wanted her to stay at home and look after the kids. That was why they had the argument, and she left the house after he slapped her. As students, we both made a vow that we would never stay with a man who dared beat us – no matter what the circumstances were, even if we had to die for it. Now, Wafa looked fragile and unsure of what to do. She wouldn't be able to remarry just like that. She wouldn't be able to run away and leave the children. She wouldn't be able to convince everyone that he was a violent man. "A slap is nothing", they were bound to say.

In this situation, the trouble was that if Wafa went back, that slap would be followed by another and another, as Mahmoud would know she couldn't leave. She would be trapped there forever. Not all men beat their wives in Gaza, in fact the majority didn't, but the problem with those who did was that society didn't have an issue with it – it was an occupational hazard of being married, a side effect that was worth suffering in order to save the health of the marriage. A woman would not go to the police to complain about domestic abuse, she would first go to her family asking for help. They would very often dismiss her complaints and tell her to return to her husband and kids, afraid of the shame it would bring them. What shame? I often thought. Was it worse than their daughter or sister taking their own life as a result?

'You are welcome to stay for as long as you want,' I said to Wafa.

'But the children? You are too far from Khan Younis, it would take me an hour just to get there.'

'Just think about it, and if you need to, of course you would be more than welcome to stay with me.'

I wasn't sure whether I wanted her to stay or not; it would be nice to have the company, but it didn't feel like the right time. So I was very pleased to see her go a week later, despite my disappointment at her decision to go back to her awful husband. While she was with me, Wafa asked a lot of questions about the investigation and Nouman and his intentions. I told her everything, as she urged me to carry on with my mission. She said that my determination to find my husband's killer was very impressive. She was a good friend giving the encouragement I needed at the time; doing her best to understand and offer solutions and possibilities.

But there was something disturbing my friend that I couldn't put my finger on. Very often she would sit on the sofa and stare out of the window for a long time. Some days, she refused to eat entirely. I assumed she was disturbed by the whole thing with her husband and wanted to go back to her kids. But one night she woke up screaming. She was staying in the spare room; her scream rang through my ears and woke me up from my deep slumber. I ran to her bed and found her shaking, uttering people's names on repeat. I thought I caught Sameeh's name, but wasn't sure. I ran to the kitchen, fetched her a glass of water and returned as quickly as possible, only to find her fast asleep.

In the morning, I asked her about what happened and what sort of nightmare she'd had, but she said she couldn't remember. I asked her why she had mentioned Sameeh, but she said she didn't know and that she must have been referring to someone else, a family member perhaps, not Ammar's friend. Sameeh was a common name after all.

Although in some respects I was pleased to see her leave a week later, I was also sad, knowing she would be suffering with that awful husband of hers and very likely be beaten up. Besides, I had got used to her company.

'If anything happens, just come here, don't worry about anything. The children will grow up and will come and find you,' I said to my friend as she finished packing her small bag.

'Wow, grow up! You don't understand, do you? I wouldn't expect you to anyway, you don't have children. How could you have your own flesh and blood grow up far away from you?'

True, she had a point, but I still felt insulted by her response. Ammar and I did not want to have children – it was our choice. But that did not mean we didn't know anything about children or the pain of those who are unable to be with their little ones. It was because of the suffering of so many children around us that we decided not to bring new ones into this world. As a child attending a UN refugee school, we had to go to a feeding centre every Wednesday to be given our ration of food. We had to queue for hours so we could get our share of pitta bread and corned beef. I grew up seeing kids developing disease because of the dirty water around us; I saw children being beaten by Israeli soldiers in the First Intifada and later bombed in a playground in the Second Intifada. I survived as a child, but I wasn't going to risk bringing another child into this world who may or may not make it through. That was the only thing I could do to help, to show my empathy for their plight. It wasn't an easy choice, but how could my friend understand?

My own mother grew up without her parents. They didn't pass away, but no one knew where they were. When the Nakba of 1948 took place and Palestine became Israel, my grandparents had to run for their lives as Jewish militia were attacking, village by village, to drive out their inhabitants. Mother was just a year old. The strategy of the armed groups was to separate those who survived. They rounded up Palestinian men in town squares and kicked out the women and children. The men were held for at least three days, chained up with hardly any food or water. Then they were kicked out to ensure that Palestinian families would spend their time looking for each other rather than thinking of returning to their homes or fighting back.

Mother was found on a road side, near the town of Asqalan, or Ashkalon as the Israelis named it afterwards. She was on her own, wrapped in swaddling clothes. Another Palestinian refugee, escaping a massacre in a nearby town, picked her up and headed towards the Gaza Strip. This refugee then became my grandfather, Abdullah Abu Daiah. My mother learned to call Abdullah 'father' of course, but she often wondered who her parents were and how they felt about losing their child.

**

Nouman still hadn't called and I was beginning to worry. On New Year's Eve 2016, I decided to walk into El Abbas police station to ask for him, to see if he had forgotten about my case. I stopped short outside his office when I saw Zakaria Abu Qamar sitting on the chair opposite Nouman's desk. He was our neighbour in Jabalia Camp. He got on very well with Ammar, and whenever we visited the family, the two of them would go out for an evening kebab at El Shaeb restaurant in the main market. In fact, very often, Ammar would check if Zakaria was at home before agreeing to go and visit the family.

My two brothers never really warmed to Ammar, who wanted to get to know Jabalia Camp and its people better. They didn't spend a lot of time with my husband, so he always excused himself to see Zakaria whenever we visited.

Seeing my neighbour at Nouman's office was a bit disturbing, mainly because it occurred to me that I had never thought of asking him if he knew anything about the circumstances of Ammar's death. Maybe I never thought their friendship was a serious one and that was why I didn't think he would add anything useful to the investigation. I thought he just kept my husband company so he didn't have to go through the normal social stuff.

'So you are telling me you only took them there and that is it? You don't know anything else? What took place there or what the two men were doing so close to the fence with Israel?' I heard Nouman address Zakaria in a commanding voice. It was the first time I had seen the detective in action, questioning someone other than myself.

'I am telling you the truth,' Zakaria pleaded.

'Let's hope this is the truth, otherwise you are going to be in big trouble if I find out you have been obstructing justice.'

I was curious to know what they were talking about, so I leant forward to get a better view, just as a policeman walked past. He stopped and asked me what I was doing there. This caught Nouman's attention, and he came out of the room almost running. Zakaria turned his head towards me and our eyes met.

'What are you doing here, Zahra?' Nouman shouted.

'I'm sorry, I came to check in with you. I wasn't sure what was happening. I'll leave now.' I looked back when I reached the door at the end of the brightly lit corridor.

'Wait,' Nouman shouted as he wrote something down. 'Take this – my mobile number. Call me tonight please.'

I hurried out, not sure how to feel. Maybe I had too much trust in Nouman, whom by now I knew I felt real desire for. I thought he felt something for me too, but seeing him in action in his own office, interrogating my neighbour, I couldn't help but think that to him I was just another case.

Chapter 9

It was New Year's Eve; we were only a few hours away from 2017. Ammar and I always enjoyed the last few hours before a year ended. We would buy lots of nuts, soft drinks and a cake, stay up all night watching films and TV broadcasts of fireworks over the pyramids in Cairo. My best memory was of 2012 – six weeks after the last Israeli attack on Gaza, when the newly elected President Morsi of Egypt interfered directly to stop the assault. We had some hope that things were changing in the region. The 'Arab Spring' was reshaping governments in neighbouring countries and Israel was becoming less free to attack us in the way they wanted to. There was also talk of opening the Rafah border between Gaza and Egypt permanently.

Wafa, Sameeh, Ammar and I stayed up until the hour struck midnight; we cheered and laughed and hugged each other. Then Ammar and I retreated to the bedroom and made love. My husband was as wild as a man who'd just been released from prison, a man who'd been deprived of sex for a long time. He made love to me, not finishing as quickly as usual. It felt as though he were on some kind of drug. I asked him to slow down and said we should be quiet, but he didn't care. He just laughed loudly and carried on thrusting, his gentle body now as fierce and strong as a charging bull. I had never been so satisfied. He didn't care that our friends were still in the living room and we hadn't even arranged bedding for them. Wafa was going to sleep in the spare room and Sameeh on the sofa.

We fell asleep immediately afterwards. I was very embarrassed in the morning but Ammar didn't seem to care; he hardly even remembered that our friends were still with us.

***

I spent the whole of that New Year's Eve alone in the flat, having bought a large quantity of nuts to keep up the tradition. I kept starting to dial 0599, then deleting it again without completing the rest of the number. My hands were trembling every time I touched the keypad on my old Nokia. I didn't know why Nouman gave me his personal number. I had the office number, I could've called him there. Did he really like me as much as I liked him? I wasn't sure, he was a very difficult man to read, but maybe detectives were trained to be – to play on people's emotions as much as possible so they could crack them.

Eventually, I dialled the number.

'Hello.' His voice was soft; not too loud or low, just casual.

'It's Zahra, sorry for calling so late.'

'Not at all, I wanted to talk to you privately and I couldn't do it in the office. Are you okay to talk right now?'

'Yes,' I said hesitantly.

'Zahra, I have been asked to drop the case. I got the call while Zakaria was in my office. Do you know why anyone would want me to do this?'

'Oh . . .' I was taken by surprise, 'Who asked you?'

'Some of my superiors.'

'I don't know any reason why. Are you going to?'

'Well, I have no other choice if I want to keep my job.'

His words killed me completely. I dropped the phone on my bed, unable to speak, tears falling down my cheeks. I could hear Nouman's voice coming through the small speaker, calling my name loudly. But I couldn't pick it up. I just stared at the ceiling as I lay on my back. I wanted the world to end then; there was not much point to it all. After a year and a half of searching, after finally finding someone who would take me seriously, the whole thing was crumbling.

I found myself lying in the same position when I woke up in the morning. My mobile phone was next to me, on silent mode, and when I picked it up I saw five missed calls from Nouman. I got up and plugged it into the charger. I could feel the dry tears in my eyes – a heavy lump that made opening my eyelids difficult. The sun was out. I made a quick cup of coffee and went to the balcony with no headscarf, and without changing my nightdress, which revealed quite an expanse of my shoulders and breasts.

Um Shihada shouted at me for appearing in public this way. 'Go and be decent, shame on you,' she said.

But I didn't even turn my head towards her; I couldn't care less what everybody else thought. If they didn't care about what I felt, why should I worry if my flesh offended people who found a woman's body far more objectionable than the whole fucked-up situation that we were in? I sipped my coffee and wished I had some poison in the house to follow it up with. I suddenly realised that trying to find the truth was what had kept me going since the war. I had nothing to live for except that. I started to think of what to do. Should I try to leave Gaza on a migrant boat? Maybe it would capsize en route and the whole thing would be over. Maybe I would get to Europe and do something with my life. Or should I just get a kitchen knife to plunge into my guts and the whole thing would be over in seconds?

I started walking towards the kitchen, and as I got closer I heard a knock on the front door. I thought it was Um Shihada coming to reprimand me. But to my surprise it was none other than Nouman. He was standing there, breathless.

'Zahra, are you alright?' I didn't answer, I just left him there standing by the doorway, turned my back and headed for the living room. He came in and closed the door. For the first time ever, I didn't really care about how I looked or whether I was dressed or not. I left him in the living room and retreated to the bedroom, shutting the door behind me. I crouched into a ball on the cold bed, reluctant to move. The first day of 2016 wasn't going as well as I had hoped. Most people would be putting their New Year's resolutions into action now, but I wished I'd never woken up to see this day.

'Zahra, come out, I would like to speak to you,' said Nouman, as he knocked gently on the bedroom door. But I remained silent. There was nothing to say. I didn't want to see him there. For the first time, I wanted him to go away and leave me alone.

'Zahra, this is important – you've got to listen to me.' His voice was muffled as I buried my head under the duvet. I heard the door open and his heavy footsteps coming towards me. I didn't even sit up to look at him, but I started crying. Something inside me was hurting so much; I felt my stomach was being twisted, as though I had swallowed something indigestible.

'Listen, there are things you should know.' He started talking as he sat down on the side of the bed. 'I think there are many things you don't know, or maybe you didn't question enough. To start with, there is no French woman called Celine. I checked all the records. I phoned a few contacts at the border control to ask about a French woman named Celine who may have entered Gaza up to six months before the war started, but I was assured the name was never on the record. I gave the description to my contacts and they are currently looking into it, but it is not easy without a photograph or any other means of identification, so it will probably take some time before they come back to me.'

I sat up and held the duvet close to me to cover my naked shoulders. Our eyes met for the first time since he came in and I saw the same kindness I found in him the first time we met. He was pleading with me to listen to him. And in that moment, it felt like he might really feel something for me, maybe he was attracted to me in the same way I was to him. It was funny thinking of this while being completely destroyed, maybe it's what happens when life collapses completely, when people are about to die.

'So, your husband wasn't telling you the truth, Zahra. Can you think of any reason why? Do you think he was having an affair?'

'No.' I said sharply.

'Very well, I am sorry. I didn't mean it that way. But the thing which puzzles me is that straight after I made the enquiry, I received the call from my superiors to tell me to drop the case. Why? I'm not saying there's a connection here but I am sure there's some sort of relationship. If you want to know what happened to Ammar, I would suggest this is the first lead to follow.'

'What about you? Are you not going to follow it up? Is this it?'

'Well, officially yes,' he said matter-of-factly, 'I want to help you Zahra, now more than ever. It just means that I will do it in my own private time and without raising too many eyebrows. I will let them know I dropped the case, but we will continue as normal. It just means we have to work smarter, without any suspicion. Have you told anyone about the investigation and what has been happening?'

'No . . . well, just my family'

'Are you sure?' Nouman stared at me.

'Yes. I didn't want to mention Wafa. I didn't want to get her involved, she had enough on her plate.

'Well, go and wash, get dressed, and we can discuss a plan. I will make us a cup of coffee.' He smiled at me as he stood up and headed in the direction of the kitchen. I smiled back, got up and carried the duvet with me as I walked towards the shower. Standing there made me think about this man in my kitchen and how much I wanted him to come and join me under the warm water. Then I got scared. I worried that my whole search for the truth wasn't really about Ammar as much as it was a search for a man. Did I even love my husband? Was Nouman right to ask if I loved him? And what was love anyway? These questions gave me a splitting headache. I got out of the shower and looked for some painkillers. Nouman came out of the kitchen with the coffee and a glass of water.

'Have you had any breakfast?' he asked.

'No.'

'Okay, well, drink this and we can go to Roots Café afterwards to get some breakfast. Oh, and happy new year, by the way.'

'You too.' I smiled as I took the coffee and sipped it. That smile he gave me, the kindness, the new year's greeting, were enough to make me feel this man was decent – that he really cared.

As I went back to the bedroom, I could hear the clattering of furniture and then the sound of a broom. Nouman was sweeping my front room, it must have been filthy. I was embarrassed. Anywhere in the world, this would be such a beautiful scene, a man being very gentle to a woman like me would be seen as a romantic gesture. But here in Gaza, this was dangerous and risky; the neighbours could start talking; word could get to my brother Jamil, who would then force me to move back to the family house in Jabalia Camp. But that risk made it even more beautiful somehow; the danger made it far more alluring, and I found myself taking my time getting ready. I wanted it to last as long as possible. When I came out of the bedroom, all dressed, wearing a blue top, a big necklace and a loose white headscarf on my shoulder, Nouman smiled and made his way to the door. We got into his car and he drove us down the Talatini Street, up towards Ansar Complex, then left towards Abu Mazen roundabout, until we arrived at the expensive Roots restaurant.

'I don't come here very often, trust me,' he said, as the waiter greeted him by name and ushered us to the table.

'Are you sure you don't hang out with all your rich friends here?'

He laughed, a deep guffaw – it really amused him to hear that. It made me laugh too. The weather was surprisingly warm; January 2017 started with beautiful sunshine; it must be this climate change. We sat outside and I lit a cigarette, replacing the smell of fresh falafel and baked aubergine with stinking smoke.

'You are determined to kill yourself one way or another,' he said, smiling.

'Are you enjoying your life, Nouman?' I asked. I looked at him with blurry eyes, feeling sorry for myself and wishing we could swap places, that I could be the one looking into people's problems, rather than facing a middle-aged man questioning me about my life.

'Well, 'enjoy' is a big word. I am okay. I am satisfied. Anywhere would have its problems. So, I wouldn't say I am enjoying it, but you know . . . '

'So, are you happy?'

'Happiness is relative. Yes, I am happy in the sense that I am not sad or angry. I am at peace, and if you define this as happiness then so be it. But I am not waking up everyday thinking 'Wow, great, this life is amazing'.'

I looked at him as he started talking. I didn't want him to stop – I wanted him to carry on and tell me more about his life, where he came from and what he had been through. He told me he was married before to a beautiful woman called Rawia. They were together for three years, when she was arrested in 1989 by the Israelis for writing pro-resistance articles in *Al Hadaf* magazine, which was part of the Popular Front for the Liberation of Palestine – the PFLP. But she passed away in prison, after developing leukaemia two years later.

'At the age of twenty-four, I became a widower,' he said, 'and a childless one. We couldn't have children. We tried everything, even went to imams who told us to read more of the Quran and gave us some essential oils and incense to burn while we were making love. Of course, it didn't help, although the sex was great as a result.'

He went quiet for a few minutes, which felt like a very long time. We ate our falafel and baba ghanoush dishes in silence. He had a good appetite and sipped his mint tea in between mouthfuls. It was a pleasure to watch a man with such love for food. Ammar never enjoyed eating so much; he ate very little and food wasn't his priority most of the time. But Nouman looked like he was having fun eating those dishes.

'So you've been single for a while?' I teased him.

'No . . . er . . . I've dated a couple of women at irregular intervals.' He looked embarrassed and didn't even make eye contact as he carried on. 'With the utmost caution, so no one in this conservative society would notice. Like me, those women were widowed too early, but for them, it was far harder to find a relationship. This society has a complex relationship with women – we respect them, we mistreat them, we love them, we hate them, we give them freedom, we lock them up – all at the same time and all at different times. Maybe you are too young to know, but the most popular saying here about how we treat women comes from a crap Egyptian comedy play which was broadcast on TV. It said that 'we' and by we, I guess the actor meant society, "lock our daughters away but we give them the key." I mean, honestly what does that even mean, but it sums up what I am trying to say about our complex relationship with women.'

'Yes, I know the saying. Everyone seems to repeat it around here like bloody parrots. They don't even understand it, but they blurt out the words as if they were good and they are doing us a favour.' I remembered how many times Jamil had said this very same saying to me, proudly.

'The first woman I dated, almost six years after my

wife died, was an amazing person. She was a hard working pharmacist during the day, working for a busy chemist in the Sheikh Radwan area. She cared for three children after her husband was killed by an Israeli assault. We only managed to meet once every three weeks or so after a lot of preparations to make sure no one knew. Her family wanted her to get married again to another man, but she refused – she never wanted to remarry, she didn't want a partner, she just wanted the company.'

He watched me as I lit another cigarette after the food.

'I often ask myself why I have never left this godforsaken Strip. I could have solved crimes around the world, more complex and challenging ones. My parents died a long time ago; I have no family in Gaza except some elderly uncles here. People here are crazy, I don't know how they can live in this desolate land. I once caught two criminals who dug a tunnel from one of the side roads coming off El Saha Square all the way across to the main municipality building. They wanted to rob the building as if it were some sort of bank. The trouble was, the idiots didn't know where they were digging, and so I didn't have to do much to catch them. It took them five years to complete their handiwork and when they eventually finished and emerged on the other side, they came up in the main foyer at 2 p.m., at the height of the rush hour, as everyone was leaving their offices. That was back in 1996, when Fatah was still controlling the Palestinian Authority in Gaza and had guards stationed in a small room at the side of the building. They belonged to the national security guards. Have you been in that building?'

He seemed to have a passion for such places. I smiled and said that I passed by occasionally but never been inside. Ammar dealt with all our household bills and accounts and I had no reason to go there.

'Maybe one day I will take you there on a tour. There are some hidden gems inside.'

'Is this why those two thieves were digging a tunnel?'

'Yes, they were convinced there was an Ottoman treasure, hidden in the building, that they could steal and then sell on. When I got there, the security guards had already got hold of them. They were loaded with maps of the building, old scriptures of the supposed treasure, which included rings of Sultan Abdulhameed II, the 34th Sultan of the Ottoman Empire. I asked them why they didn't just go for the Arab Bank next door instead. They looked at me in shock when I asked, and one of them said, "There is a bank there?" Then he looked at his companion in anger. I mean how stupid do you need to be?'

Nouman laughed deeply and I too found myself giggling really loudly.

'Some people are so thick,' he continued.

'So, is there any treasure or not?'

'Why? Are you going to dig a tunnel yourself?'

'Well, if things get bad, maybe.'

He laughed and stared at me for a while.

'Well, Sultan Abdulhameed refused to sell Palestine to Theodor Herzl, the founder of Zionism, who wanted to build a Jewish state here back in 1882. The Sultan was aware of the Zionist colonial intentions and made sure to prevent this, travelling often from Turkey to Palestine, making it very difficult for Zionist European Colonialists to purchase land in Palestine. It is said he stayed in Gaza a number of times and that he left some of his belongings somewhere. Some believe these still exist and they are kept in the municipality building. I think if they really did exist then they would have definitely been either destroyed or stolen by the Israelis.'

'Damn, so no treasure then!'

'Well, maybe we should go looking for it too,' he said. 'I will show you around.'

'Deal.'

Nouman looked at me then and his smile started to fade,

'On a more serious note, I think . . . hmm . . . er . . . how should I put this? Well, I think you are right. I think your husband was murdered and not killed by an Israeli airstrike.'

I was speechless. For the first time since that awful night someone agreed with me, someone actually understood what I was talking about, someone was taking me seriously.

'Since taking on this case, a lot of strange things have happened,' he carried on. 'For example, your being followed and assaulted.'

'You know about that?'

'Of course,' he said. 'Although your doctor's report was useless, he couldn't determine if it was an attack or not. Then someone tried to get into your family house in Jabalia Camp, but not your flat in Gaza City.'

How did he know all of these things, I wondered? But then he was a detective, he must have his ways.

'Are you tailgating me, Nouman? Am I a suspect too?' Oh god, he was just another detective.

'No, of course I am not. It's just that my office helper happened to be at El Shifa Hospital and he told me that he saw you.' We remained silent for a while.

'And to answer your question, everyone is a suspect at this stage. Then there's Celine, the most interesting of all. The mysterious, allegedly Frenchwoman, who took your husband away three days before he was killed, and who turns out not to be French and not called Celine.'

I was silent, completely shocked by all these things, although he had already told me about them. I felt my head spinning.

'And to top it all off, one of my superiors has asked me to drop the case. Why do you think that anyone would want us to stop looking into this? There is something I don't understand here. From what you have described, Ammar was the most peaceful man, who had no enemies whatsoever; a dreamy person, living in a fantasy world. Why would this be a threat to anyone? But then there are a lot of things that you are not able to answer.'

'Like what?' I asked, with tears in my eyes.

'You said he didn't speak to many people during the lock-up period. Have a look at this.' He pulled out a piece of paper from the inside pocket of his jacket.

'This is his Jawwal mobile statement. I managed to get it through a contact of mine. I gave them Ammar Bseiso's name and address and they emailed this to me. Do you recognise the top number? It seems he texted it many times.'

'No. Let me put it in my phone to see if it comes up.' I typed in the number, but I didn't have it saved.

'Well, any idea who your husband might have been texting?'

'I have no idea, Nouman . . . I have no idea . . .' My tears started to fall.

'I am sorry, this might be shocking to you. But I need you to focus more. Where is his mobile phone?'

'I don't know, I've never looked for it.'

'Why not?'

'I didn't think of it.'

'Okay, so you were informed your husband had been killed in an Israeli attack on a house in Shujaia, where there were four other guys plus your husband. You went to the morgue in El Shifa Hospital–'

'He was wrapped in a white shroud,' I interrupted. 'They gave me a plastic bag with his belongings in: a brown leather wallet, his ID card which was burned, his watch and our wedding ring.'

'But no mobile phone?' Nouman asked quickly.

'No.'

'And you didn't ask them?'

'No.' I felt very stupid as I lowered my head.

'Okay, Zahra, listen. Here is what I want you to do. When you go back, I would like you to go through all your belongings and find any mobile number that might have been written on a piece of paper – collect everything that might give us a lead as to whose this number is. Go through your paperwork since you got married; let's see whether or not we can find a clue.'

'Have you tried calling it?' I asked with almost certain knowledge of the answer.

'Yes, of course, it is off all the time.'

'Nouman, does this mean you are still taking my case?' I asked desperately.

'Well, of course I am, but I am not going to make any noise about it. For now, I will keep as quiet as possible and I would like you to do the same. Someone out there has sensed that we are digging into it and they are trying to stop us – we need to be as discreet as possible. Don't talk to anyone about it unless you trust them fully.'

'Okay,' I said, half-happy he was still working on the case and half-scared of what was to come. A big part of me wanted to simply drop the whole thing and escape completely, but I was too far into it now. There was no way back. Maybe I should've listened to Jamil and stopped early on, accepted the whole thing and not bothered to pursue it.

'We will also have to be discreet in our meetings for now.'

'What, you mean like having an affair?' I was trying to joke a little to lighten the mood.

'Not exactly, Zahra. How about we meet at the municipality building from now on?'

'Only if you show me around?'

He smiled as he waved for the waiter to get the bill. We stayed silent for a while, as though the conversation had dried up completely.

'It will all be fine, Zahra, I am sure.'

That kindness almost killed me. He always had the perfect words for everything. This ability to jump between the kind human being and the sharp detective was the most attractive thing about him. When he smiled and looked at me in that way, it made my body temperature rise. I felt terrible, because here I was fancying the person who was investigating the death of my husband. Was that too weird, too sick?

Perhaps I should have pushed my luck, let Nouman know how I felt, opened up an alternative opportunity. Then I could have turned this into a romantic breakfast instead, run away with him and forgotten about the whole thing. Why didn't I do that? Well, maybe because of the guilt, and my loyalty towards Ammar, but also my curiosity to find out what had happened. It wasn't about my dead husband anymore, it was about proving I was right and that everyone else who had called me crazy was wrong, particularly my stupid brother Jamil who was against the whole thing from the beginning.

Chapter 10

I found myself searching through the flat for all our paperwork, looking for anything that might lead me to that cursed number which Nouman wanted so badly. I searched the bedroom thoroughly, going through every single piece of paper which might offer clues. We had lots of old photographs from university, particularly from the time when an American delegation came to visit us on a summer school programme. We had fun with them: photos of scorching sunshine on the beach; barbecues; playing football. We studied cultural programmes about the 'American Dream' and I remembered how one of the students was really shocked to learn I knew about jazz music.

And there I found one of my favourite photographs, of Ammar in his majestic role as Richard II in the final production of our Shakespeare assignment, the one we had constantly rehearsed. I remembered how my husband didn't like the royal robes that our low budget costume designer made for him. He complained to our professor that it didn't look kingly enough, so he went out and bought an Arabic Abaia and gave it to the designer to create new majestic robes for him. The poor thing worked for days until she produced something that looked perfect, but it still wasn't good enough for Ammar.

In the photograph, he was standing stage left, upright, facing me, with his back to the rest of the cast. He had a big smile on his face as he was about to banish Henry:

> *With harsh-resounding trumpets' dreadful bray,*
> *And grating shock of wrathful iron arms,*
> *Might from our quiet confines fright fair peace*

> *And make us wade even in our kindred's blood:*
> *Therefore, we banish you our territories:*
> *You, cousin Hereford, upon pain of life,*
> *Till twice five summers have enrich'd our fields,*
> *Shall not regret our fair dominions,*
> *But tread the stranger paths of banishment.*

Shakespeare's words sounded so sweet coming from his mouth, as he tried to be as regal as a fourteenth-century English monarch. It somehow suited him; he was full of life and arrogance. Perhaps that was why both he and Richard II ended up as dead as a worthless worm. I looked more closely at the photograph of the king. He was almost staring back at me. His face was full of happiness, not knowing what the future had in store for him.

I refocused on the task Nouman had given me, but there was no mobile number of any kind. I threw the photos down on my dressing table and went to our smaller second room, which we mostly used for guests. We had kept it tidy and clean. There was a small bookshelf with the Oxford Dictionary on it, as well as an English-Arabic Dictionary and a few books from university days. I went through the shelf, opening the books to make sure there was nothing inside them. I looked around the single bed, but there were no papers there. The last time I tidied it up was the previous week, when Mother had come to stay. I bent down and looked underneath the bed. Still no papers. But as I was about to stand up, I noticed something black in the far right-hand corner, next to the leg of the bed. I lay on my stomach and stretched out to retrieve it. When I stood up I was shocked to see I was holding a Motorola mobile phone I had never seen before. It was very dusty. I tried to switch it on, but there was no battery life. There was only a Nokia charger in the house, which was the same make we both used. Still, there was a small glimmer of hope that the phone belonged to someone else. Mother could have dropped it when she last stayed, but then I had never seen her use this handset before. Or maybe it was Wafa's and she'd accidentally left it here when she stayed with me.

As I stared at it, I felt scared. It was then when I realised things were going to be different, that I was a fool living a complete lie, that the man I loved was not the one I knew and that he kept so many secrets from me. For some reason, the news that Celine wasn't real didn't scare me as much as finding an old mobile phone in the house. I wasn't sure why that was, but somehow the betrayal felt too close to home. Something inside my stomach churned; I was sure this handset belonged to Ammar.

I didn't want to know what was on that phone. I looked at it for a long time and thought how stupid I was, not to have noticed that my husband had another mobile. Why would he need another phone? What was he doing?

Then, out of the corner of my eye, I saw her in a picture on top of a pile of papers on the floor. There she was, but with a different hair colour. Celine had long black hair in the photograph, but I was sure it was her. She was part of the American delegation that came to El Azhar University on the summer programme. We had both spent a lot of time with the group – in study skills classes, research activities, cultural programmes, taking them out in Gaza, and even visiting my family home in Jabalia Camp. How had I not recognised her to start with? What an idiot I was! She was part of the group, but we never spoke. She was one of those who stayed on the fringes of large gatherings, hardly any personality at all. Sure, she had changed since 2000, she had long black hair back then unlike the blonde short style she had when she came to our house three days before my husband's death. But it was the same smile, I remembered it.

I felt as though I was about to faint. I couldn't stay in that house any longer. How had I not recognised Celine? And what was her name anyway? Well, what was the name she used as an American student? I couldn't remember. Wafa would remember, for sure. She had a good memory, and I was certain, if I asked her, she would be able to tell me. Then I could take it to Nouman and tell him all about it. I rang Wafa, but she didn't answer. I tried again and she picked up the phone, breathless.

'Hello,' she said.

'Are you okay?' I asked, 'Is your husband home?'

'He just left.'

'Wafa, listen to me. I need you to answer a very important question.' I gave her the description and told her everything about Celine and the photograph I had just found. She listened, said she couldn't remember, but that it should be in the records of the English Department at El Azhar University, and surely Nouman could get them to give him a copy of the names and all their details.

I couldn't stay in the house any longer. I grabbed my Nokia phone, the Motorola handset and the photographs, and left immediately. I started walking as fast as I could without any real direction. I went down to Omar Mukhtar Street, to El Jalaa Street junction and walked down the long road all the way until I got to Sheikh Radwan neighbourhood.

The scent of oranges filled the air, wafting across from a couple of farms in the nearby Jabalia Town. Subconsciously, I was walking back home to Jabalia Camp. I headed down El Saftwai Street all the way to El Twam Street, then took a right towards El Fakhoura, and before I knew it I was descending on Jabalia Camp. People were sitting outside in the warm weather, soaking up the sun. For some reason, I felt everyone was staring at me. Citrus scent was quickly replaced by petrol. There were donkey carts waiting outside the UN Refugee Centre as people waited to get their rations, and when I got towards El Markez Police Station, the stinking smell of a large bin on fire made me pinch my nose hard.

As I walked near the Girls High School, I phoned

Nouman and told him everything I had found. He couldn't see me, but he asked me not to go back home or to my family's. He asked me to go to a friend of his in Tel El Zaatar, and said he would come and find me later that evening. The problem with that plan was if my family saw or heard from one of the neighbours that I had come to Jabalia Camp without telling them or stopping by, I would be dead. So I had to zigzag through the Camp's narrow streets to avoid seeing anyone I knew. I took a left before I got to El Markaz, turned around the water pump, past Abu Rashid's water reservoir, then all the way to El Trans Street, up the hill onto Abu Khousa Street, then left on Tel El Zaatar.

Abu Suleiman opened the front door and ushered me in. He had a large five-storey house that overlooked the Jabalia Camp. He took me up to the roof and offered me a cup of sage tea. He asked me if I needed anything and told me to consider this my house at any time. I didn't quite understand why Nouman had sent me there and what I was doing, and neither did Abu Suleiman. He had grey hair and a grey beard, although he looked much younger than Nouman. He had a wife and six children of different ages and sizes. They all ran to me to say hello and looked in bewilderment because I was wearing jeans and a tight top with a loose headscarf.

'You are in the Camp now,' he said. 'You will be very conspicuous in this outfit. I can get you a *jilbab* to throw over if you like.'

'Thanks, that would be great, I left in a rush.'

He whispered something to his ten-year-old son, who rushed downstairs in a flash.

'Have you always lived here?' I asked.

'Yes, since my father was deported from our village near Jerusalem in 1948. We were one of the very first to come to this area. The first official refugees.' He spoke with a smile which hinted at a modicum of pride, as if there was any in being a refugee. He seemed to be a very kind man, a family person, playfully hugging his youngest thirteen-year-old daughter, whom he introduced as Princess Yasmin. We sat in the sun on the roof, sipping our tea. There was some comfort in that setting. The sun was shining on some tall buildings across the way, which looked like a huge line of washing hung out to dry. I could almost see steam coming out of the buildings. Refugee camps always looked drab in Gaza, and maybe everywhere, but every now and again, colours came out through the sunshine, reflecting off the solar panels used to heat water. The Camp could look magical with different reflections from the rooftops, as if some spiritual force existed there.

Or perhaps it was simply memories being squeezed out of people. Those memories evaporated whenever winter settled in: whenever sewage flooded the streets; whenever people lined up at the UN Refugee Centre waiting for their food rations; whenever the Israelis bombed us. You could almost see those memories steaming up from the tops of the houses, high above the big black water tanks, like souls rising up to heaven. But then, a wedding party would start roaming the streets, with men drumming loudly on an old pickup truck, followed by a huge line of cars all pressing their horns as hard as if it were the apocalypse, kids running behind them and women ululating loudly. And then life would be revitalised. "Just like a phoenix", Ammar would surely say.

'How do you know Nouman?' I finally asked.

'Well, we were in hospital together. We shared a ward. He was on the bed next to me for about a month.'

I kept silent, wanting him to say more, but he was waiting for me to ask questions.

'Were you ill?'

'No, neither of us were. We were both shot; I by the Israelis, and he by a drug lord. It was at the beginning of 1994, as the Israelis were stepping up their arrests and shooting at the Palestinian resistance in preparation for the arrival of the Palestinian Authority. They wanted to make sure that this damn authority would get a grip over Gaza and do their dirty work for them.'

'I take it you are not a fan of Fatah then. Are you Hamas?'

'These are all names, just names. Don't be hard on judging Hamas yet, they are doing their best. I am not a member, but I admire their spirit of resistance, the way they tell the Israelis to fuck off, the way they have always invented new ways to resist, which is our right, or any nation's right. I believe in resistance. The Israelis have taken everything from us, everything – even hope. What's left?'

'Your children and family,' I said abruptly.

'Well, yes, but do you really think they have a future here?' He spoke as a truly disappointed man, a man who had thought about the situation. I'd thought him to be a family man who had nothing to do with political activism, but I was wrong. He now looked more like a retired soldier who was trying to make his family his whole life. I could see that deep down there was something inside him which hurt him terribly.

'Maybe things will change,' I said, trying to comfort him.

'Perhaps for the worse. You saw during the last assault in 2014; the Israelis burned everything for us, even the will to live. There are those who disagree with me, of course, and I respect their views, but for me, I feel no one will come to help us – no world leader to enforce a peace settlement; no neighbouring country; nothing. If we don't resist and stand up for our rights, we will soon perish. Palestine will become a collection of small communities encircled by a majority who will never give us our civil rights. This is a white man's world, my daughter, and we hardly count – they don't even see us. Anyway, how do you know Nouman, and why has he sent you here?'

'Er . . . he is looking into a case for me. My husband was killed – I mean murdered – and someone tried to cover it up and claim it was an Israeli attack. Today, I found out some more information about it and he asked me to come here instead of going back home. I have no idea why.'

'I am sorry to hear this; I hope it can be resolved soon. But let me tell you that you've got the right man. He's an honest person. He will be very straight with you. Nouman loves his job and there is nothing in the world he adores more than catching criminals. Sooner or later, he will catch them for you. I have no doubt about that. I have learned a lot about all his adventures chasing criminals in Gaza. You would think there wouldn't be so many people committing crimes here given how small the place is, but there are always those who try to take advantage of any lack of order.

'During our time in hospital, lots of families of victims came to visit him. His wife had just passed away so he was still grieving.

'I blamed him for working for the Blue Police, which was effectively under the direct control of the Israeli army, but he was not bothered about that. He thought better a Palestinian detective than a foreign Israeli occupier, who would just commit more crimes than the criminals themselves. He also assured me that the force was completely independent. This is when I came to trust him. The Israelis were waiting for me to heal so they could take me to prison – a soldier was stationed outside our ward. But Nouman got me out, through some contacts who came to visit him. When I was able to move, he asked his young cousin to come with a group of women wearing black dresses and *niqabs* to cover their faces. He also asked him to bring a spare dress and *niqab* for me. I put it on as they prepared to leave and we all ran together out of the door. You see, the Israelis didn't dare search a covered woman, but that was back then. Now, they do anything they bloody like. And that's how I escaped the Israeli prison, by dressing up as a woman.'

Abu Suleiman talked of Nouman as if he were his own

brother. There was pride in the way he described the detective to me. They spent a lot of time together after the Israelis evacuated their soldiers from Gaza. Abu Suleiman came out of hiding then, and through his connections he managed to stay low key under the watchful eye of the Palestinian Authority, who were arresting anyone who thought of resisting against Israel.

Nouman and Abu Suleiman visited each other weekly – apparently. Nouman liked the little Akkela Falafel Restaurant and loved to have a Barrad ice cream at Abu Zaytoun at the corner of Madaris street. The two of them became inseparable.

I had only known Nouman for about ten days by then, and I felt as though I had learnt a lot about him already. For some reason though, the idea that he was a workaholic bothered me. The fact that he dedicated so much of his life to his work was a little off-putting. Despite how difficult life in Gaza was, work was always considered as a means to end, a way to earn money so you could enjoy life. People visited each other a lot, cherished gatherings on long summer evenings. A trip to the beach with its rustic, palm-covered little huts was the ultimate pleasure; a wedding party on the street drew hundreds of passers-by, and even watching the Egyptian football league made people cheer themselves senseless.

Gaza was a simple place to live, still innocent in some ways, still growing up and maturing into a world which had moved on too fast and left our little town in the slow lane.

When the July war broke out in 2014, my brother Issa was watching a football match broadcast live, all the way from Brazil. When I asked him why he was paying attention to football in such terrible times, his response was that war came every two years to Gaza but the World Cup came only every four years. That was my brother, just a simple person from Gaza, and he and many of his peers laughed in the face of death, they cheated death and sometimes even befriended it.

But Nouman was someone who focussed a lot on his work, as though trying to progress in his career. Maybe he wanted to advance to a higher position. The feeling that both he and Ammar were very similar came back to me – they were both deluded. He wasn't the perfect guy I had hoped he was.

I began to daydream about us going out together when this whole thing was over, maybe getting married and living together at some point. It was wrong of me to think like that, but I couldn't help it. I found him very attractive, but what I had learned about his obsession with work was less so. Being in his fifties was also worrying, but he had the energy of a man in his twenties. I never thought I would find another man attractive. I was content with Ammar, full of love and hope for the future. I never even admired or felt any desire for another man.

***

We stayed on the roof for a long time. Abu Suleiman's wife, Um Suleiman, joined us and we had a late lunch together around 3 p.m. when it started getting cold again.

I didn't know what to do. Nouman still hadn't turned up and he had asked me not to leave his friend's house. We went downstairs. There was no electricity. The house was very cold, but Um Suleiman handed me a thick blanket and her husband started burning some charcoal in a barbeque container to generate some heat in the living room. I chatted with his six children and asked them about university and which subjects they studied. I helped his youngest daughter, Princess Yasmin, with her English language homework. They were very grateful and impressed with my English.

By 8 p.m. I could almost sense the horrible feeling of outstaying my welcome. The kids lay on the rug covered with thick blankets, huddled near the charcoal grill, Um Suleiman was staring at me, and her husband was listening to the news on a handheld radio. The streets were pitch black by then, with hardly anyone moving. The whole Camp was falling asleep. My eyes were shutting, when I heard a loud knock on the door. Abu Suleiman got up very quickly, lit another candle and made his way to the front door. I wanted to follow him to receive Nouman by the door and ask him why the hell he was late. But women were not meant to open front doors in the Camp, so I waited until I heard my host's voice calling me to come to the guest room and to bring another candle.

I put on my headscarf and the *jilbab* I had borrowed from Abu Suleiman's family and went to receive the guests. Nouman was crouching down on the thin mattress on the floor, laughing with Abu Suleiman. I went straight to him as he stood up, shook my hand and introduced me to someone sitting next to him. The man got to his feet immediately, almost knocking over the candle next to him. I could hardly see his features in the semi-darkness, but he looked very young.

'This is Samer, he works with me and is responsible for our technology department.' I looked at this young man, sizing him up, and as if Nouman read my thoughts, he continued. 'Don't be fooled by his age, he is young, but quite a wizard with the old technology.'

'Very nice to meet you,' I said, as I stared at his big, wide smile.

'Can I see that mobile phone please?' he replied quickly, while still shaking my hand. I took out the old Motorola handset from my pocket. He tried to switch it on immediately, but of course it didn't work. Within seconds, he was sitting down on the mattress again. He grabbed a black laptop bag next to him and got out a charger; he searched through numerous cables and found the right one to plug it in. He then got his laptop out, switched it on, removed the phone's battery but still kept it plugged in so it would work, then he attached a small wire to the back of the phone and connected it to the computer. A black screen appeared and he started to scroll through.

'Are you in?' Nouman asked sharply.

'Of course, did you doubt it?'

'Good man,' Nouman responded. 'When was the phone last used?'

'19th July at 16:25 precisely.'

'No . . .' That was just thirty-five minutes before Ammar left, how could that be possible? The only phone I had seen him with was his usual Nokia, I had certainly never seen this new and mysterious phone which had suddenly appeared in my house.

'Zahra, are you okay? Do you want us to do this another time?'

'Absolutely not . . . now, I want to know everything now.' Um Suleiman came towards the room and called for her husband to come out and take the tray of mint tea she had prepared.

'Come, please sit next to Zahra, she could do with your company.' He ushered his wife in, and she started handing out the small hot cups.

'Okay,' Nouman said, 'I need you to focus now. This will be difficult, but try to please.'

'Okay,' I said, and Um Suleiman held my hand as she crouched next to me. I looked at her and suddenly saw kindness I hadn't spotted before, as if she understood.

'A phone call or a text message?' Nouman was staring at Samer, waiting eagerly for an answer. Samer took his time to scroll through the black screen.

'Phone call,' he answered, then started reading the number aloud. Automatically, I got my phone out and asked him to repeat the number, and the colour must have drained from my face.

'It must be a number you recognise, you've gone pale,'

Nouman said in a soft voice.

'It's my brother's number – Jamil. There must be a mistake here, are you sure it's Ammar's phone?'

'We can't be sure,' Nouman said, 'but it seems likely. Samer, can you check the SIM card to see if it's registered against someone–'

'Already done,' said Samer, before Nouman finished the sentence. The IT geek looked at both me and Nouman without saying a word. He knew and understood. He looked down at his screen again.

There was silence for a few, very long seconds. Nouman looked at me with glassy eyes, expressionless, not sure what to say. The revelation shocked him as much as it did me. He didn't need to ask any further questions; he guessed that Jamil hadn't told me that he had spoken to my husband an hour and a half before he was killed. Was this why Jamil never wanted me to find a detective to look into Ammar's death? Was this why he got angry when I told them I had found Nouman? But why? And what did they speak about? What happened in those last few hours?

'So, why did he send about fifteen text messages from his other mobile phone, the one I know about? Why didn't he use this one?' I asked impatiently. Everything was very confusing, nothing made sense anymore.

'I don't know,' Nouman answered. 'Maybe this phone ran out of battery and he had to leave in a hurry. My guess is that he hid the phone when it ran out of juice. Remember, he didn't know what was coming, so he probably thought it was a mistake he was able to afford at the time.'

'What number is that?' Samer asked, and Nouman got out a piece of paper and handed it to him. He started scrolling through, typing very quickly on his keyboard, as we all looked at him in anticipation. Even though I was eager to find out, I was afraid of what was coming. My whole life was on the line there; everyone in the room was learning details about my husband that I didn't know myself. I felt like a fool.

'Although this number starts with a 0599 Jawal code, it is actually connected to an Israeli phone number on the Orange network, but I am afraid that's as far as I can get, given that it is a different company. I can't access any further data,' Samer said, while continuing to look at the screen.

'I think you should stay here tonight,' Um Suleiman said, as she held my hand tighter.

'This is a good idea,' Nouman said. 'Samer and I will leave now and let you rest for a while; I will be in touch.'

They were both up on their feet before I could say a word. Nouman held out his hand to shake mine and I suddenly remembered the photographs, so I just handed them over to him. He looked at them for a brief second and then turned around and headed for the door. Samer followed him like a puppy. I wanted to go home, but words were not coming out, I couldn't protest against the decision that was made for me. Once again, I was powerless, almost imprisoned again in this strange house, my brain trying to work out why my bastard brother never told me that he spoke to Ammar shortly before his death.

The room was suddenly empty. One of the two candles was burnt almost to the base. After the guests left, Abu Suleiman announced that he was going to sleep and his wife would sort me out with bedding. When she re-entered the room, she wasn't carrying a duvet or pillow, but was dressed to go out.

'Come with me,' she whispered. 'Let's go out for a walk, clear your head a bit.'

I was surprised; it was getting late, cold and dark outside, and women didn't wander alone at night in this conservative part of town. But without uttering a word, I put my shoes on and followed her to the door. The wind was crisp; the warmth of the day had disappeared completely. We walked quickly through dark streets. The power cut had blanketed the entire area in darkness. Although it was only 10 p.m., the whole of Tel El Zaatar seemed very quiet. I could hear a dog barking in the distance, a stray cat jumped as we turned right heading up the hill. The smell of cooked tomatoes, fried aubergine and chips, a typical Gazan dinner, was coming out of one of the houses. We kept zigzagging through little streets filled with houses built with fragile cement bricks and asbestos sheets for roofs. Graffiti filled the walls of almost every street we passed through and I could see the faint pictures of people martyred in the last war on Gaza. I realised I hadn't walked through this part of Jabalia Camp for a long time. The landscape had changed. There were now open spaces with nothing in them except rubble. Entire streets brought down to dust. I wondered where the people were. Um Suleiman and I were two ghosts walking through a haunted place.

'Do you walk here often?' I asked her to break the silence.

'Well, sometimes, to take a break from the great touristy sights Jabalia Camp has to offer.' I laughed and held her arm. She was my guide, leading me through my own town which I could barely recognise. We got to Sikka Road and she stopped for a while, watching the bright light coming from the Israeli watchtower on the other side of the fence.

'Once, there was a train here that used to connect Gaza to Egypt and Haifa in Northern Palestine, and onwards to Beirut. This is why it is called the Railway Road. If you look carefully, you might spot parts of the old track built by the British when they occupied the land.'

I was fascinated by her knowledge and didn't expect it for some reason. When I first met her she looked like a typical passive woman – mother of six children, dominated by her husband. But now she was a tour guide, a historian who was taking me on a magical trip and – much to my shame – I didn't even know we had had a railway at some point.

'Yes, my father was the conductor,' she carried on, as though talking to herself, recounting a memory of happy days. 'I loved the train rides with him. We used to go as far as Jerusalem, and all the way up to Haifa and Beirut. In those days, Father used to turn a blind eye to a lot of people who didn't have tickets. From the age of six I started to meet so many people travelling up and down the country. That was before the Six Day War, when Israel officially ended the service. Once we checked the tickets, my father would give me some money to buy him a cup of coffee and sweets for myself. I used to run to the small canteen and rush back to Father's little cupboard room, which was filled by a massive radio and a small chair and table. He would sit there and listen to the soft voice of Um Kulthum singing at the top of her voice through the speakers, bringing the whole of Egypt to Father's train. He would be so happy just reclining and resting his chair against the wall. The music was too boring for me. I would run out and wander between the aisles, chatting to people, telling them all that my father was the train conductor.

'One day I met a little boy, sitting next to his blind and deaf grandfather. He was the same age as me and I wanted to play with him. I remember my delight at finding him. I hadn't realised how much I was eager for kids' company on that long journey. But he wouldn't leave his seat. His grandfather had his arm around his shoulder. He remained silent and didn't even respond to my requests. We were only eight years old then, but at that moment he looked like a little man. I ran back to Father's cupboard room and brought some old photographs of the two of us in Cairo and Beirut which we'd taken on some of our journeys. The boy didn't even glance at them, he just stared ahead.

I kept returning, bringing snacks and sweets, leaving them on his lap and running away. And just before the journey ended, as we were passing this very same Sikka Road, coming back from Egypt towards Jerusalem, he told me that his name was Jamal and that he was accompanying his grandpa back after spending a few weeks in an Egyptian Hospital in El Areesh. I told him my name, Aida, and said I would always look out for him near the train station in Jerusalem if he wanted to come and see me. And he did, often, indeed for many weeks afterwards. Jamal is none other than Abu Suleiman.'

She stopped talking and started walking very fast as we reached the junction between Masoud Street and Salah El Dein Road, which runs all the way down to Rafah in the south of Gaza. As she picked up her pace it felt as though she was going to walk all the way there. I smiled as I tried to catch up with her, thinking of the innocent little girl she was then, and the romantic person she became. Did we really have true love stories in Gaza? Were they our own Romeo and Juliet? She married the person she loved as a child. How did they make it happen? Did their families just agree? I wanted her to tell me more, I wanted to hear her story and escape mine completely.

'We became inseparable friends between the ages of eight and twelve, then he disappeared when the service was stopped in 1967. We could not get to each other. I begged Father to ask for him, but we had no way of knowing where he was and how to reach him. We were already refugees in Gaza and he was from Jerusalem. There was a big fence between us.

'When I finished high school, my father refused all marriage proposals from my suitors and insisted I should go to Beirzeit University in the West Bank. He wanted the best education for his daughter, and it was in the second year that Jamal – Abu Suleiman – and I were reunited. He was studying law and had already been an active member of the student union. I recognised him immediately when I saw him address a crowd of students, encouraging them to join the cultural resistance and write just like our great writer, Ghassan Kanafani, who was killed a few years later.

'I walked towards him as if I were in a Bollywood film. He hadn't recognised me at all. I reminded him quickly and we embraced in front of everyone. We still held to our innocent selves. Everyone stared at us even though Beirzeit was far more liberal than Gaza.

'We became very active together and we got into so much trouble, but we were never arrested. We dodged bullets, Israeli military jeeps chasing us, other spies informing on us, and a host of other things. I wrote many anti-occupation articles in the university's magazine. I was studying Arabic literature at the time.

'Then, we got word that all of our friends who were active in the resistance had been arrested, so we had to escape. Someone arranged for us to leave the West Bank and head into Jordan. We walked endless hills until we reached Amman, and from there we travelled down south to Aqaba, then crossed to Saudi and later to Egypt. The whole journey took around two weeks, in between hiding and running. We bribed our way through.

'We got to Cairo, but Jamal was very depressed. The life of the big city did not suit him and he was dying to go back to Palestine. But the only option we could think of was to go back to Gaza, rather than the West Bank, as we knew it would be impossible for us to go there. We made our way through the Sinai desert and when we got to the border with Gaza, we went through a big dusty tunnel that let us into this damned Strip'.

She was as old as my mother, yet looked much younger; she had something about her, an energy which surrounded her. Despite the darkness and lack of electricity, she knew every corner we turned. She walked with confidence, without watching her feet, as if she had made this journey many times before.

'You are surrounded by two good people, Zahra,' she suddenly said to me.

'What? Sorry?'

'Nouman and Abu Suleiman.' I wish I could have seen

her face at that moment.

'Should I trust Nouman?' I asked instead.

'Do you have any reason not to? Take my number, call me at any time! You are alone, let me know if you want to talk things through.'

I saved her number on my phone. Then we turned back and walked in silence. I looked to my right as we walked back on Sikka Road. The eastern side of the Jabalia Camp was lit as if it were daylight. The Israelis had fired balloon lights, which were as bright as the sun. They often did this. We would see night change to day in an instant with the firing of these awful military inventions. The whole area was silent; half of it drowned in the darkness where we walked and the other half basking in the light.

When we got back, Abu Suleiman was sitting outside the house. He looked at us from a distance and seemed to have recognised us despite the dark. Um Suleiman quickened her pace, but did not say a word. He was sitting on one of the three half-broken steps which led to his front door. It was cold, but he had wrapped a *keffiyeh* scarf around his head and put a thick blanket around him. He was smoking slowly, staring at the wall opposite him as if it didn't exist.

'Nouman phoned for you! He woke me up, the bastard.' Abu Suleiman was looking at me as his wife put her hand on his shoulder, and I checked my phone and saw three missed calls from Nouman.

There was something about this couple that was so soothing, so comforting, that I didn't even care what Nouman had to say; I just wanted to watch these two lovely people who had gone through so many hopes and failures in their lives. For a split second, I imagined the two of them as kids, full of hope for a better life, travelling together on a train between Egypt and Jerusalem. What a world that must have been. Her hand was still on his shoulder and I couldn't decide whether they were still living the life they once envisaged or not. It felt to me that Abu Suleiman had given up on life a long time ago, but that his wife was still hanging on to it, the same way she still held on to his shoulder, the way she held on to her memories, still a child trying to hold onto a seat on the train or the ticket machine, helping her conductor father.

'He asked me to tell you to meet him at Gaza's municipality building tomorrow morning, as soon as it opens at 7:30 a.m.'

'He's keen,' murmured Um Suleiman.

'Well, it must be important – otherwise, he would've found another time. He also asked me to accompany you.'

Chapter 11

I couldn't sleep that night, still in shock to hear that Ammar had called Jamil just before he died, and that my bastard brother had never mentioned it. Why would he do that? I also couldn't wait for morning to come so that I could see Nouman. He was the only one now who had all the clues. I shared a room with Um Suleiman, who fell asleep instantly, the moment she lay down on the foam mattress on the floor, covering herself with a duvet and a very thick blanket. She was snoring like a train, perhaps dreaming of that very same train she used to ride.

My main concern in the morning was how to leave Jabalia Camp without being spotted by any of my brothers or their families. Abu Suleiman wanted to walk down from Tel El Zaatar to El Trans Road in Jabalia Camp to catch a cab to Gaza City, but I insisted on him going and bringing a cab to the door, so I could sink into the back seat without being spotted. He did just that, with an added treat of a fresh falafel sandwich and a cup of sweet mint tea, which he handed to me as soon as I got in the car and waved goodbye to Um Suleiman.

Her husband sat in the front passenger seat, said his *assalam aleikom* to the driver and fell silent, unlike many men in Gaza who seem to strike up a conversation with a stranger in the blink of an eye. The driver didn't look very impressed by his unsociable passengers, but he kept his eyes on the road and sped ahead. I put my head down and wanted to cry – I was so afraid. I didn't know what was going to happen from now on. I had let the genie out of the bottle and had no control over it anymore. I couldn't even make my three wishes. What else was in store for me? I started remembering the number of times Jamil had told me off for trying to find a detective. I felt his voice ringing in my ears, telling me it was a stupid idea: that I was wasting time trying to find who killed my husband; that it would all lead to trouble; that I was crazy and needed a mental hospital instead. Maybe he was right. Maybe I should have left things as they were; it wasn't as if Ammar would have come back from the dead anyway.

But I was not only afraid of what had happened or what I was going to discover. I was also scared of the man whose murderer I was trying to find – yes, my very own husband. He had suddenly become a stranger, a new person with another phone, a different circle of friends, conversations that I was not part of. They could have been talking about any other random person, but not my Ammar. I remembered once walking with him down this very same road, on El Trans Street, going down the centre of the Camp. There used to be a café, just by the taxi station near El Markaz Police Station. It was mostly men smoking *shisha* there, but we went in a few times and smoked too.

It was a lovely evening. It was very warm in late July, but a cool western breeze from the Mediterranean made it pleasant, despite the noise of beeping cars, braying donkeys, and the cooking gas seller who kept banging on a gas canister with pliers and had some weird music playing like an ice cream van. The place was filled with the smell of apple flavoured tobacco burning in *shishas* everywhere. At 9 p.m. on such a beautiful evening, the Camp was brimming with life. Kids were walking shoulder to shoulder – discussing politics, of course – and then the call for prayer made everyone pause whatever they were doing, as if a remote control was pressed before the hustle and bustle returned.

On that very evening in 2004, when Ammar and I were still engaged, he told me that we should always be open with each other and tell the truth no matter what. He said that if I ever discovered he was lying to me about anything, no matter how big or small, I should walk away and not look back. I thought he was being overly dramatic and teased him about it, but he was not impressed. He looked dead serious. He was staring at me hard, so I blew him a kiss and smiled.

That night we made love passionately in the new flat we'd bought together and which, funded mostly by his rich parents, we were still doing up. There wasn't any furniture yet. We got a couple of take away *shawarma* sandwiches and two Diet Cokes from Abu El Abed in El Saha and took a taxi to the flat on Talatini Street.

We weren't meant to be alone in the flat, despite the fact we were engaged.

'People will talk,' I said to him, as he stared at me, undressing me. I felt his warm hands on my shoulders as he unfastened my bra, then gently touched my breasts. He was indeed a gentleman, he never rushed a thing. He caressed my body for a long time before he too undressed, and we made love passionately on the floor. We lay on our backs in the empty flat and looked at the ceiling, smoking cigarettes and dreaming of a future that looked so bright ahead of us.

***

Now, that evening felt different, as if it had been a setup, a big trick, a trap which I fell into. Did he really mean what he said? Did he know that one day I would discover his lies? But why? And what were they? The man I shared a bed with for a long time was not the man I knew; he was a different person, and it frightened me.

Suddenly, I remembered Zakaria Abu Qamar, who was being interviewed by Nouman the other day. I realised I hadn't had the chance to think about it and why he was there in the first place. Before going to see Nouman, I wanted to get more details, I wanted to understand more, to feel in control again and not leave the whole thing in his hands.

The car came to a stop for a moment near Khadamat Jabalia Sports Club, where Zakaria's house was, behind a little corner shop where he used to hang out in the evenings sometimes. Without thinking, I opened the door of the car, jumped out and started running. Abu Suleiman was shouting at me to come back, but I didn't slow down or even glance behind at him. I turned right into a small unpaved alley, splashing through a big puddle of water coming from a leaky pipe outside one of the houses.

It was too early to knock on Zakaria's door, so I kept going, from one alley to the next, going around in circles and trying my best to avoid being spotted by my brothers, their wives or children. I kept walking, heading down one alley after the other, cursing the way this Camp was built. They all looked the same, dozens of houses with grey unpainted cement bricks. The whole place was like a maze. Most of the houses didn't have roofs, but just a few asbestos sheets that covered the temporarily erected walls, placed on top of steel poles. The sheets were littered with stones to stop them from flying away in the cold winter. Those houses were useless, I thought – boiling hot in summer and freezing cold in winter; a tiny upgrade from a tent.

As it got to 8 a.m. and I got tired of walking, I decided to head back to the Sports Club and find Zakaria. I didn't know what I would say to him or why I was going to see him in the first place. But just as I got back to the main El Juron Road, very close to Zakaria's house, I saw her. My mother was standing there looking straight at me, as if she had been there all the time, waiting for her little daughter to come back. My heart dropped; I had been a bad daughter and hardly asked after her.

***

The thing with my mother was that she was one of the kindest people ever, and most likely the calmest human being you could ever meet. Despite all the destruction around her, she had a calming effect on other people, a gift which that demanded respect and authority.

But for that very same reason she could sometimes appear passive, not quite there, not engaged in things that made me angry or passionate. As a teenager, mourning the death of my father, who was the complete opposite to my mother, I learned not to share my emotions with her because she never engaged with them. She never understood what it meant for a teenage girl to lose her father, to lose her first love for a man. To her, it was a matter of practicality: how to make the funeral arrangements; how to keep Issa and Jamil emotionally strong; what they needed to do over the three days of mourning; who was going to get the bitter black Arabic coffee; who was going to light the fire, rent the marquee and plastic chairs; buy the dates and cigarettes to hand out to people; which Imam was going to read the Quran.

I thought it was her way of coping, that after the funeral was over and everyone had left, leaving her to her pain and agony, she would come to me – she would hug her only daughter and maybe cry. And she did, after she stopped being mechanical about it, sorting out father's debts and collecting money that people owed him. She came to my room ten days after the funeral; I was lying on my bed staring at the ceiling. She sat beside me, started stroking my arm, and I smiled at her. Then, she hugged me tightly and cried for a long time; she sobbed like a baby, letting go of all those emotional masks she had previously worn. I didn't know what to do. I couldn't cry as that would have made her worse, so I started singing to her – a song that Dad always sang, and whenever he did we knew he was in a good mood, that we were getting a treat that day.

> *Wa Hada El Bulbul El Roman*
> *Smieto Bil Leil Yeghani*
> *The nightingale landed on the pomegranate tree*
> *I heard him at night singing*
> *It woke up my little one who was happily asleep.*
> *The nightingale was visiting the groom next door*
> *He said to him: think no more, your bride is the best in*
> *town.*

Mother joined me in singing; the words sounding nasal as the tears jammed up her voice, remembering a time when father came home and he was so happy. He was singing at the top of his voice, we didn't know what was happening. He was just happy. So we all started singing, Jamil and Issa clapping hard while providing the male chorus to the song, and I ululated. Some of the neighbours knocked on our door to find out what was happening so they could celebrate with us. But there was no news or party, it was just a happy moment, stolen from amongst the struggle around us. That night, Dad went out and bought lots of freshly made kebabs from El Shaeb Restaurant in Jabalia Camp central market. He also sent Issa to get us the mouthwatering sweet *kunafa* for dessert.

Dad was very generous in lending people money whenever they needed it. He was a contractor in Tel Aviv, taking a lot of Palestinian workers into Israel to do construction jobs, cleaning and farming in the days Israel allowed us to work in our stolen land for money. I asked father about this many times. When I was nine years old, I wanted him to explain why he worked for the people who colonised our lands and made us refugees in the first place.

'For two reasons, my clever daughter: one, because we are not allowed to build factories and make our own economy succeed here. We can't have heavy industry or import stuff without Israeli permission. The second reason, which is far more important, this land is ours and we want to look after it, whether it is governed by us or by people who come from Russia. The land is the same; she doesn't change. She knows us and we know her – she is our mother.'

I thought of his wise words. At the time they felt magical and romantic. The way he referred to the land as 'she' was innocent in a way, almost sentimental.

Now, all of that was gone, as no Palestinian workers were allowed into Israel anymore. They were replaced by new Thai, Vietnamese and Filipino workers instead.

After my father's death, my mother became the boss temporarily, until Issa was old enough and strong enough to become our second father. She handed over managing the family affairs to him and became very passive in the family – well, certainly with me. I often wondered what would have happened if we had got on a little better, if we had become friends.

My parents got married slightly later than was the habit in Gaza in the 1970s. Dad was still in his early career as a builder in Israel. Zuheir El Tanani was a handsome man who spent his whole week away in that ugly new city called Tel Aviv, while mother taught maths in a local UN school. She had studied at Cairo University, which was unprecedented for a young woman from the Gaza Strip, but her adopted father let her follow her dream. Despite her four brothers' protests, he paid for her education and made sure she had comfortable accommodation in his cousin's four-bedroom, 1930s flat in El Zamalek, a posh neighbourhood in Cairo.

They met when my father came into the house of Mohammed Abu Daiah, mother's father, to give a quote for building a second storey. Mother often said that she fell in love with Father the moment he walked into the house. They were engaged quickly, and in 1974 Issa was born, seven years before me and three years before Jamil.

***

That morning, on the second day of 2017, my mother was standing there on the corner of the nameless alley where Zakaria lived. She was waiting for me, hands crossed, staring with unfocussed eyes. Nouman's and Abu Suleiman's instructions were not to let anyone know my whereabouts. I slowed down to see her expression better, but as usual, she didn't display any emotion – she was such a hard woman to read. I hurried towards her and we embraced. She felt very warm in the morning chill. She towered above me, stroking my hair, while hugging me tightly. It was exactly what I needed. I had to cry, I had to let out all my stress.

'Mother, what do you know about how Ammar was murdered?'

The question seemed to startle her, and she pulled away from me.

'As much as you do,' she replied after a moment's thought.

'Do you know what I know, what I've learned over the last couple of days?'

She shook her head and stared at me, encouraging me to continue. But something told me to stop and not tell her I knew Jamil had spoken to Ammar hours before he was killed, that my husband and brother had a strange relationship which I could not understand, that there were some dealings between them. I looked at her eyes for a long time, trying hard to decide whether to tell her or not, but I couldn't. I had to trust Nouman – I could not spoil it, not then, not now.

'How come you are here, Mother?'

'I could ask you the same question; you live in Gaza City and you came all this way, at this hour, without telling us. What are you doing here?'

Her question startled me. I didn't have an answer, a credible reason to give her for why I was in Jabalia Camp at 8 a.m.

'I came to see Nouman. He is at El Markez today and asked me to come over. So I came a bit early.' I had to think on my feet but I knew that mother wasn't convinced. She just nodded.

'Let's have breakfast,' she said, and started walking without hesitation or waiting for an answer.

We walked back to the main El Juron Road, past the Sports Club and all the way down to the police station in El Markez, past the UN Centre for Refugees. A lot of people were queuing already, with their blue UN cards that allowed them some rations. Sacks of flour were being loaded on donkey carts, ridden by kids no older than eleven years old. Others were leaving the queue loaded with gallons of vegetable oil, dried baby milk and cans of corned beef. Everyone in Jabalia Refugee Camp had a blue UN card that allowed them some basic supplies – our supposed compensation for losing our homes and land in 1948.

We walked down to El Merkaz Square, turned left and started climbing the hill towards El Fakhoura Girls School. Abu Ismail's Humous & Falafel Restaurant was very tiny and modest; only a couple of plastic chairs and a small table stood in what looked more like a corridor than a restaurant. He wiped them down for us and immediately brought a couple of cups of mint tea without us having to order. The smell of mint was very comforting, I held the small cup in both hands to warm them and let the scent penetrate my nose.

'Listen to me, daughter,' she said sharply, as she put down her cup of tea, 'I have never stopped you doing what you wanted, but this is getting out of hand.'

'What is?' I stared back at her. 'Do you know something I don't?'

'I don't know anything, but I can guess. I can see through things more than you think I can. Strange things have begun to happen since Nouman started interfering. I have no doubt that his intentions are good, but I don't trust anyone anymore.'

'Mum, why are you saying this? Why can't you understand me? You have never tried to understand how I feel.'

'I do,' she responded sharply, 'I do, but you refuse to see it.'

'Are you trying to protect someone?'

'Someone? Who? I am disappointed in you, Zahra.'

Abu Ismail brought some hot falafel and a bowl of *foul* beans for us with freshly baked bread, chilli sauce and olive oil. Without even asking us, he poured the chilli sauce on the humous. It made me smile when I saw customers saying they didn't want chilli on their food – the faces of the café staff were always a picture, as though they couldn't believe what they'd just heard. When I was at school, Mother always made us chilli sandwiches for lunch. Sometimes she added a dash of olive oil and lemon if she was feeling generous.

Abu Ismail placed everything on the table without saying a word, as if he understood how tense the conversation was. He also brought two cans of 7-Up for some reason – another eating habit in Gaza which I never embraced.

'I need to find out who killed my husband, Mum. I made this clear to everyone ages ago; I am not going to stop now. I am sorry, I know this is not important to you, but it is to me. I will not stop, not now.'

'Even if it leads to worse things?'

'Like what? That's what I don't understand. You keep saying these things without explaining. Why won't you tell me, why won't you speak to me like all mothers speak to their daughters?'

I was shouting by now. Luckily, Abu Ismail had a queue of workers who were half-asleep, waiting for their falafel sandwiches. He was too busy taking orders to pay attention to us, but a few of his customers stared at me as I raised my voice.

'I don't have anything to explain; I just have a feeling. It's the years I've lived in this Strip that make me realise this is leading to trouble. Stop it right now, I am telling you to do so. I am begging you from a mother to a daughter to just put it behind you and start your life again.'

'I am sorry, this is not up for discussion and no one can tell me what to do.'

The silence which followed was painful. Her words and mine hovered above us. We could both see the effect of what we'd said to each other and that, from then on, our relationship was going to be different. She was not the disinterested mother anymore, she was trying to stop me from doing the one thing I wanted to do right now – finding out who killed my husband. I took out ten shekels from my purse and placed the coin on the table. She pushed it back towards me. 'I am still your mother, put your money away.' The coin fell off the table and rang loudly on the floor. A kid from the queue ran and picked it up and helpfully handed it back to me.

'Let's start again, my daughter. We lost so much in this damn war – let's not lose each other. We are still here, we are family.'

'Well, then let me do what I want to do. Please, Mother.' She fell silent, swallowing back her tears.

'Someone has come asking for your hand in marriage – a customer at Jamil's blacksmith workshop. Jamil has convinced Issa to accept. They will be coming tomorrow to read the Fatiha Verse announcing the acceptance.'

'You must be kidding me,' I shouted as I got up. 'Goodbye, Mother, tell them to fuck off. I don't want a husband and certainly not one that Jamil has pimped for me.'

She was silent for a while, staring at me as if I had just confirmed to her what a total waste I had been as a daughter. I couldn't usually read her thoughts but the look on her face said it all – she was disgusted.

I sat back down. 'I am sorry for the rude choice of words, but Mum, listen to me, you and Dad married because you loved each other. You didn't go the traditional way, why should I?'

'But you married Ammar out of love, your way, and look what happened?'

'Yes . . . I didn't tell him to get killed, though. I am sorry, Mum. Try to understand me a little. I am not intending to get married at the moment and I know this will upset Jamil, but he's got a few things to answer first.'

'What does that mean?' Mother asked sharply.

'Mum, there are things you don't know. For instance, has he ever mentioned to you that he spoke to Ammar only an hour and a half before he was killed? Why do you think that was? And why did he never think of mentioning it to anyone, particularly to me?'

She was silent again, staring past me as though I wasn't there.

'There must be a mistake, that can't be true. Why would he do that?'

'Well, that's what I am trying to tell myself, but, Mum, we found a phone, another handset and SIM card which Ammar apparently used on many occasions. The last call that was made on that line was to Jamil and they spoke for approximately fifteen minutes.'

I could almost see a tear falling down Mum's cheek, but she held herself together, took a deep breath and looked away, staring at the little falafels being thrown into the hot oil.

'See, my daughter, this is not going to end well at all. Things will only get worse. Is Nouman now suspecting your brother?'

'I don't know, Mother. To him, everyone is a suspect, including myself. There's also Sameeh who claims that he and Ammar stopped being friends, but I know they didn't because I saw them together. I also saw Zakaria being interviewed.'

'Zakaria, what, that idiot who's a complete waste of space?' Mum said, with a big smile on her face.

'Yes, Mum. In fact, I am here to see him. I wanted to ask him what he talked to Nouman about before going to see the detective.'

'What, are you a detective now too? See, my daughter, you are going insane!'

'I am not, Mum, trust me. But my whole world has collapsed around me. The man I knew, or thought I knew, is not the same man who was killed. Ammar had so many dark secrets and I want to know what was going on. I think I used to be a fool, but not anymore. I want to know everything, even if it costs me my life.'

She stood up, preparing to leave, and left the coins for the bill on the table. She was smiling at me. She didn't complain any further; she just nodded as if giving me the go ahead to carry on.

'Be careful,' she said, before she shot off. I wanted to stop her. I still had so many questions for her. How did she find me in the Camp that morning? Was it a complete coincidence?

Suddenly, I felt sad she had gone; I felt as though I wasn't going to see her for a long time. I felt like running after her, I loved her so much and wanted her to stay with me all day. But instead I turned back and went to see Zakaria.

Chapter 12

I ran out of the restaurant and headed back down El Fakhoura Street and took a shortcut next to the medical centre at the back of the UN Refugee Relief Centre. I zigzagged through a few alleys, until I found myself behind the sports club where Zakaria lived. It was 9:30 a.m. by then and the sun was blazing, warming the streets. I loved winter sun in Gaza. It could be very warm, and always gave me hope, filling my head with the thought that spring and summer were on their way. I knocked lightly and a small child opened the front door. He appeared to be around six years old and had a big smile on his face. He invited me to come in, but I asked him if Zakaria was home. His mother's voice rang out from behind him asking who was at the door. She came out, still fixing her white headscarf around her head on top of her nightgown. I explained that I was there for Zakaria. She seemed surprised but invited me to go in and wait in the living room, which had mattresses and cushions on the floor. I took off my shoes and entered reluctantly.

Zakaria came in a short while afterwards, wearing a long jellabiya which he used as pyjamas. He smiled a wide smile. His teeth looked as clean as ever, he still had the same designer stubble, and his hair was even curlier than before. His eyes had the same shine, and he looked so handsome when he smiled. Zakaria fancied me when we were at high school. He used to study at Usama Bin Zeid High School, and after finishing his classes, he would run as fast as possible to wait for me outside El Fakhoura Girls School, where I used to go. I liked him a lot but I was never into him; he was never my type. Besides, he was my brother's friend and it was too risky to start a secret relationship – Jamil would have killed me. He looked taller than I remembered, but then again, I hadn't seen him for many years. Ammar liked him too; they met when Zakaria came to see Jamil in the family house in Jabalia Camp. For some reason, lots of men came to visit that day, and as was the habit I had to leave my then fiancé to sit with strange men he had never met, evacuate the guest room for them and go to the living room to sit with the guests' wives.

'Zahra, what a surprise! *Ahlan Wa Sahlan*, welcome,' Zakaria said.

'Thank you,' I said as I shook his hand, really wanting to give him a big hug.

'You've met my sister-in-law, Ridda, I believe,' he said as she brought a cup of mint tea – although I really wanted a coffee. 'And this is my little nephew Ayman, the best nephew in the world.'

'Thank you, Ridda. Yes, Ayman looks so clever.'

'Go and play outside.' Zakaria pointed to Ayman, who wasn't happy about being ordered around in front of a stranger. Ridda went back to the kitchen.

'What brings you here, Zahra? Sorry I don't mean to be rude, but I am surprised – it's been ages.'

'Yes, it has. I am sorry that we didn't keep in touch, but I believe my husband did the job for me.'

'What job?'

'Keeping in touch? What happened to your IQ, man?'

He laughed his usual high-pitched laugh as I teased him.

'Well, clearly non-existent, as you can see.'

'Not a problem, it must be difficult with family and kids.'

'I can't claim that excuse I am afraid, still single as ever. Anyway, how can I help you?'

'Help me?' I said. 'Blimey, that's formal.' Zakaria was a medical receptionist at the UN Medical Centre, and sometimes his polite manners extended to his social circle too.

'Sorry, didn't mean it that way.'

'Well, I think you know why I am here. I should have come ages ago, but I was waiting for the right moment.'

'Until you found a detective you mean, who has been interrogating me already?'

I was shocked to hear him say that.

'I don't blame you,' he carried on, 'I would've done the same too, but I am afraid I don't have much to help you.'

'How do you know? I haven't even asked anything yet?'

'No, yes, sorry, go ahead.'

'All I wanted to know is how close Ammar and Jamil were. I mean, did they actually like each other?'

'Zahra, do you realise how silly this question sounds coming from the sister and wife?'

'I know, I am sorry. But lately, I am discovering that this sister and wife knew nothing and may have been living in a different world altogether.'

'Hmm . . . like what?!'

I wasn't ready for him to ask questions; I was there to ask, not answer.

'I am sorry, I can't say, it's private,' I responded quickly.

'Well, the answer to your question is, I don't know. It was very pleasant every time we met when Ammar was down in Jabalia Camp. The two of them would come and fetch me and we would go to the same *shisha* place, smoke loads, talk about politics, football, and sometimes women. Then I left them to their own devices. It was just normal, I never had the chance to ask them if they liked each other, but they certainly didn't seem to hate each other, because otherwise why would they hang out?'

'You are closer to Jamil than Ammar. Has he ever told you anything about Ammar that made you wonder a bit?'

'What, are you turning into a detective now? And if you are, then you need further training, what kind of question is that? I have no idea, what do you mean by making me wonder a bit?'

'Zakaria, please . . . I need your help.'

'With what, Zahra? In the last few days, I got called to a police station and now you turn up like this . . .'

'I don't know, I really don't. I honestly have no idea, I am sorry to disturb you.'

My tears started to fall as I gathered myself ready to leave.

'Wait, I know someone who may help you understand things better . . . erm . . . well I don't know him personally, but I heard Jamil and Ammar talk about him very often. He's a farmer in the El Soudania area. He's got a little plot of land near the fence with Israel, in the north. We can go and see him if you like – his name is Abu Eyyad.'

'What makes you think that he will be able to help?' I asked quickly.

'Well, I don't know if he will, but I am trying to think of all the people who knew the two of them together and if they could give us any information.' Zakaria looked at me, embarrassed, as if he was keeping some secret. Of course I had no choice but to follow this new and unexpected lead – some strange farmer in the most northern part of Gaza that I would have never thought to even consider. Why would I?

'Have you told Nouman about him?'

'No, he didn't ask and I didn't think to mention him either.'

We set off through Jabalia Camp again, by this time I was getting sick of all the alleys and streets that I seemed to have circled all morning. I asked Zakaria to stop a taxi that would take us to the farm. I was also worried that I would bump into Mother again or one of my siblings.

The taxi sped through El Fakhoura Street, up towards El Saftwai Street and carried on towards El Twaam roundabout where we turned right on the beach road and carried on all the way up north, until we could see the fence with Israel. An Israeli military jeep was visible in the distance. I was worried that they would start shooting at us, as was often the case when they saw something move near the fence.

The driver asked us to be careful, took his money and promised to come back and pick us up in two hours.

We walked across the uneven ground. The land wasn't ploughed well. I could still see the marks of military tanks, which had left wide prints of metal chains on the muddy earth. Zakaria explained that Israeli soldiers often invaded here whenever they liked without any excuse. There was an uneasy feeling about being there, surrounded by soldiers and guns. Despite the fact that we were still in Gaza, it felt like we were somewhere completely different – a closed military zone, perhaps. We continued walking until we spotted a shed in the distance. Our instinct was to head towards it. Zakaria didn't know where he was going but had assumed the leading role somehow.

'I have missed you, Zahra,' he said suddenly.

'Well, thank you, Zakaria. How come you never came to ask after me?'

He started sweating as he looked for words. I was taking pleasure in seeing him so confused, I felt something inside me come back to life.

'Well . . . I couldn't, you know, a single guy making contact with a married woman in Gaza is an unforgivable crime . . . especially when this married woman is the sister of my friend.'

I laughed at this remark. Of course, I knew full well that he couldn't, but I wanted to tease him more.

'But you mentioned once that you liked me so much.'

'I did . . . I do, but I couldn't. Maybe because I liked you so much, I didn't want to make life hard for you. In any case, you made your choice and got married and never gave me a chance, so why should I bother anyway?'

He seemed somewhat angry then, but still looked ahead, focussing on the shed.

'I know, I am sorry, I was only joking. It's been a whirlwind, as you know.'

'That's an understatement!' He laughed, and sped up.

Suddenly, a strange feeling came over me. Zakaria and I were taking a journey into some farmland by the beach, which was by any standards a romantic walk, and I felt I was betraying not Ammar, but the man I had so many feelings for – Nouman. My mother always told me that a woman's love for her man was eternal, that women were very different from men in the sense that their loyalty was difficult to shake; that men could quickly move on with their emotions, but women couldn't. This was part of my mother's ten tips for a successful marriage, just before the wedding night. But now, I felt all that she had said was untrue. In just under two weeks, I had stopped loving Ammar and was easily falling for another man, someone who had not been part of my life before, with whom I had no history. Maybe it was the feeling of wanting to start again; maybe it was the fact that Ammar had betrayed me in such a manner that having an affair would have been much easier to bear, and maybe it was because I was being liberated once more. I no longer felt I had the burden of finding my husband's killer. I wanted to do so for myself now rather than for his memory.

There was nothing in the shed when we got to it. There were just a few haystacks to the side of the cracked wall, a burned pot of tea was lying on the untiled floor and a broken plastic chair was by the door. It was about four metres square in total. The roof was made out of thin metal sheets that stood on badly made grey cement walls. The whole thing looked like a bunker from World War II. It smelled very salty, as it was very close to the beach.

Zakaria and I looked at each other and smiled, knowing that we had no other plan. We didn't know where Abu Eyyad lived and we had two hours to spare before the taxi driver came back to pick us up.

'We could walk back to the main road and try to find a cab?' I said to Zakaria.

'You've become such a city girl that you've forgotten that taxi drivers prefer to pick up passengers rather than Israeli bullets. Why do you think I paid twenty shekels for the driver to get us here? Because no one else would come out here.'

'Okay, stop your rant,' I said, jokingly, 'it was just a suggestion.'

He smiled again, smoothed his curly hair with his right hand and looked at me.

'What if you find out something you don't like? Will you still want to know the truth?' he asked, as he stared at me.

'Yes,' I said, without a moment's hesitation.

'What's the truth worth? Why is it so important?'

'For my sanity, that's why it matters.'

'Zahra, I liked you a lot before, I like you even more now. Maybe this is why! Maybe because I would do exactly what you are doing right now. If someone killed my wife, I would certainly want to know who did it, even if it cost me my life.'

'Finally, someone understands,' I said jubilantly.

'I thought your detective did too, this is why he agreed to take on the case.'

'He does, he did. Well, I am not sure anymore, to be honest.'

'What do you mean?' Zakaria said quickly.

'Well, he was asked by his superiors to drop the case. Strange things have been happening. I was followed down the street by a creepy stranger, and an intruder seems to have got into my family's house in their absence and searched for something.'

Zakaria was listening intently.

'What do you think they wanted?'

'I don't know . . . a . . . a . . . phone maybe.'

'Phone?!' he said sharply. 'What phone?'

'Never mind!'

'What do you mean "never mind"? You have to tell me everything. You've asked for my help and I brought you here, so I need to know the full story.'

'Why do you need to know?'

'Because I can help you.'

'How can I trust you?'

'Well I didn't come to you, did I? You came to me. There's the door, walk out right now, leave, never come back to see me and consider that this morning never happened. I am not going to stop you.'

He was pointing at the door as I looked at him. He had the kindest look in his eyes. I found myself telling him everything: all the mysterious circumstances around Ammar's death; our lock-up at home; the strange French Celine woman; the phone; being followed and knowing that Ammar and Jamil talked just a few hours before my husband's death. Zakaria listened intently, scratching his designer stubble every now and again and responding with "yes" and "I see" frequently, but without offering any opinion.

'Do you trust your detective?' he asked, when I finished.

'I don't have any reason not to, Zakaria; he was the only one who believed me and, as I looked for you, I went looking for him.'

Zakaria was still staring at me intently. 'I don't know, Zahra, I feel as though you shouldn't trust him for some reason. You might have gone to him first, but perhaps he has found out something that he's keeping secret. I don't believe this thing about his superiors wanting him to drop the case. Why would they do that?'

But before I could answer that, an old man walked into the shed with the help of a walking stick, accompanied by a silent old black dog.

'*Assalam Aleikom*,' he said in a hushed croaky voice, as he entered. He was wearing a long dark *jellabiya*, with the *keffiyeh* scarf wrapped around his neck. He had a long face, with a bushy white beard. There were only a few teeth left in his mouth.

'*Wa aleikom assalam*,' both Zakaria and I responded in unison, which made us smile.

'Have you come here for work? I am sorry there's not much work left in this land. You better try somewhere else.'

'No, we are not here for work,' I said instantly.

'I used to have lots of people coming here for casual work, but since the Second Intifada the Israelis have destroyed all my olive groves, so there are no more olives to pick.' He looked as if he was about to embark on a long story.

'Are you Abu Eyyad?' Zakaria interrupted him.

'Yes, I am, the owner of this wasteland. And you, who are you? What's your name? *Mashallah*, you have a beautiful wife!'

'She is not my wife. She is a friend, we've come to ask you some questions, if that's okay with you. My name is Zakaria and this is Zahra.'

'First names only don't make sense to me, tell me your family names. I am bound to know one or two of your family members.'

'I am Zakaria Abu Qamar and this is Zahra El Tanani.'

At the mention of my name, the old man looked me in the eye.

'I know why you are here,' he said to me, without looking at Zakaria. 'I am sorry, I can't help you with anything.'

'Help me? Who said anything about help?'

'Then why are you here?' He was getting agitated; his dog moved in a circle too.

'I want to ask you a few questions about my brother, Jamil El Tanani, and my husband, Ammar Bseiso.'

'Oh, that spoiled rich city boy. Sorry, I don't know anything.'

'How do you know him then?'

'I don't,' he said sharply.

Zakaria moved to the corner of the room and grabbed the broken plastic chair, he tested it to make sure it could still seat someone, then carried it straight to Abu Eyyad and ushered him to sit down.

'Have a seat, uncle, you must be very tired.'

He sat down, and his dog rested on the floor beside his right foot. He started stroking it.

'What is he called?' Zakaria stroked the dog too.

'Ghadab,' said the old man.

'That's a funny name for a dog. Is he always angry?'

'Well, he used to be when he was a puppy.'

'I see,' said Zakaria, as the old man calmed down. 'Listen, uncle, we didn't come here to make trouble, in fact the reason we are here is to save any future trouble. You may have heard Ammar is dead now, he was killed in July 2014. He wasn't killed by an Israeli strike, but someone murdered him. There's a detective looking into the case right now and he is about to figure everything out. He works for the government, you know Hamas people, although I understand he is not one of their members. Nonetheless, he has powerful contacts whom you may not want to upset.'

The old man stared hard at me, it was as though he was blaming me for the whole thing. He looked as confused as I was.

'I think you can trust us more than him,' Zakaria continued, and I marvelled at his ability to calm people down.

'What do you want to know?' he asked, while still looking at me.

'Everything,' I said.

'That's an exaggeration,' Zakaria said quickly. 'We only want to know how you know Ammar and Jamil. That's all.' My brother's friend and my former fan winked at me, and I stopped myself from talking again.

'Well, they used to come here often. I don't know why, but they said they liked it here. They would sit in this very same shed and just chat.' The old man spoke while stroking his dog. He took something out of his pocket and fed it.

'And you never asked why? Or what business brought them here?' Zakaria asked.

'No . . . never. I liked them both – well, Ammar got on my nerves a little with his city behaviour. He really didn't get the hard working life, be it as a refugee or a farmer.'

It was weird to hear someone talk of my dead husband this way; he clearly didn't like Ammar, but then I too had started to dislike him then, or dislike the person I was getting to know.

'Okay,' Zakaria said, and I was grateful that he was there doing all the talking. 'What did you, or they, talk about?'

'Well, you know – politics, the state of things, we drank tea . . . that's it.'

'Did anyone else ever join you?' I started to be impressed by Zakaria's detective abilities.

'No . . . hmm . . . no . . . yes . . . I'm not sure.'

'What do you mean?' Zakaria asked.

'Well, no one came when I was here, but I often left them to it. I thought they wanted to be alone, and I carried on working on another part of the farm.'

'Did you ever see anyone else while they were here and you were working, or not with them?'

The old man scratched his head for a long time. He took a silver case out of his pocket and started rolling a cigarette. I watched intently, every second felt like an hour.

'Yes, a couple of times, or maybe more. Once I saw someone wearing a police uniform heading towards the shed shortly after I left it. Another time I remember seeing the two of them walk towards the beach with a woman who was not wearing a headscarf and who looked foreign. A strange thing happened once. They were walking close to the fence with Israel and I hurried to follow them to stop them from getting so near, in case they got shot at. But I stopped dead when I saw a black car approaching them; my eyesight wasn't good enough to figure out the model. Someone got out of the car and spoke to them for about twenty minutes. It seemed like an argument, they were waving their hands in the air and walking backwards and forwards. Then both parties retreated back to their positions. I thought it was the strangest thing I'd ever seen. I didn't know the fence had an opening there and I wasn't sure how the car got through.'

'And you never asked them about it afterwards?' I interrupted.

'No, I only saw them once or twice after that. Jamil and Ammar were arguing as I entered the shed, their voices were very loud and I couldn't understand anything. I tried to calm them down but they wouldn't, so I left them to it. The second time, they had an old white Peugeot car and they were loading boxes in it. I greeted them and they said they had come to give UN donations to the local area. They asked for recommendations of people who needed help and I gave them a few names.'

'That was the last time you saw them?' Zakaria asked.

'Yes. I wondered why they'd disappeared. I missed their company a lot, but then the war started and everyone kept to their own as you'll appreciate. I didn't have a number to call them, and I hoped they would return after the war, but they never did. I was once in Jabalia Camp selling herbs in the market when I saw Jamil walking down by the stalls. I stopped him and asked him about Ammar and he told me he was killed by an Israeli strike in Shujaia. I am sorry my daughter, I can only imagine how painful this must be for you.'

He was looking at my tears, which had started to run heavily by then. I couldn't stop them. I wasn't sure why I was crying. The mention of my husband's death was always difficult, but what was even harder was that I seemed to have missed all of this. I was oblivious to things that Ammar got up to. I felt guilty for not asking enough questions, I felt stupid and cheated, I felt undermined, fragile, angry and, above all, scared. I didn't want to hear more, that was enough. I started gathering myself, ready to head out; I could hardly breathe. Zakaria noticed and started chatting to the old man in a low voice, perhaps thanking him for his time. I was already out of the door when my friend joined me.

'Are you okay?' he asked as he took hold of my left arm. I snatched it away from him and just carried on walking, quickening my pace but not sure where to head to.

'Stop . . . stop . . . Zahra . . . please . . . Let's just talk it through, let's make a plan. Let me take you for lunch, there's a nice fish restaurant at Jabalia beach, let's just walk there and we can eat some food at least.'

I didn't respond, but I followed him willingly. I wasn't hungry, I had no appetite, but I knew that I had nowhere to go. I couldn't go back to my flat, I didn't know what would be waiting for me there. Nouman would have been searching for me now, given I had missed our meeting. I couldn't go to Abu Suleiman's house for the same reason. I couldn't go to my family's house after the argument with Mother this morning, and I certainly didn't want to see Jamil's face and confront him. The bastard; I could kill him. Why hadn't he told me all of this? Did he kill Ammar? The thought made me physically sick, and before I could stop myself I leant towards the cactus bushes on the side of the sandy road and threw up.

'Feeling better?' Zakaria asked after I had finished and rejoined him.

'Sorry about that, I am not myself.'

'I can imagine.'

A thought occurred to me – why not go to my eldest and wisest brother, Issa, and tell him everything? He would help me for sure. After all, he had assumed the fatherly position in the family. And, as if he could read my thoughts, Zakaria stopped.

'Let's not make any decisions now, please Zahra – let's just talk it through.'

We carried on walking for about twenty minutes until we finally found the little restaurant on the main Jabalia Beach. It was scruffy and dirty but the smell of the salty air coming from the sea was very refreshing. The owner explained that they didn't maintain the place well in wintertime, as they didn't have many customers.

But then another thought came to me. I excused myself to go to the bathroom and quickly got out my mobile phone and texted Um Suleiman. She had given me her number last night and asked me to call her if I needed anything.

'I am at Rantisi Fish Restaurant, come and get me please if you can. It's urgent'.

I made sure the message was sent, switched off my phone and put it back in my pocket. I don't know why I did that. There was no immediate danger; I had no reason not to trust Zakaria, but maybe I had lost all trust in everyone. All these men around me were pretending to be brave, pretending they knew what they were doing, but they were as scared as mice. They were full of lies and deceit. But what were they scared of? I couldn't tell. Not just yet anyway. There I was having a romantic fish lunch on the beach with someone who used to fancy me, learning about how deceitful my dead husband was, while waiting for a woman I had only met the night before to come and rescue me from something I couldn't see.

'Zakaria, you have known Jamil for such a long time. You've been very good friends since childhood. Why do you think he hasn't told me any of this?'

'I don't know, Zahra; I wish I had a better answer.'

'So he claims he never liked my husband and never got on well with him. Yet they met in secret and did some dodgy stuff together. What's this all about?'

He didn't answer to start with, then looked at me as if bringing together all the thoughts from the labyrinth of his brain.

'What's all this about the foreign woman? You mentioned something about her, and Abu Eyyad just said that a foreign woman once met them. Who is she?' Zakaria asked.

'It could be Celine – the supposedly French woman I told you about, who turned out to be an American study-abroad student whom we met in Gaza in 2000. I wanted to ask Abu Eyyad about her, but with his eyesight he wouldn't have recognised her features from a distance. But I am certain it is the same person, who else could it be?'

Zakaria was silent and looked as if he was thinking about the whole thing. I wasn't sure what was going on in his mind but he smiled at me occasionally as I started eating. There was something uneasy about the way he looked at me and, for the first time, I felt exposed. I'd told him everything, giving him all the information I had without withholding anything. I started to panic, unsure whether this had been a good idea or not, and what Nouman would say. I was sure he wouldn't be impressed.

Thinking of Nouman made me feel sick. I felt as though I had betrayed him somehow. He was the only man who'd believed me in the first place and who was on my side – or at least said he was. I liked him so much and wanted him to like me. Yet here I was, sitting with someone else who clearly didn't like my detective, who had declared his feelings for me and, on top of that, had started acting like a detective himself.

Everything was muddled together and I didn't know what to do. I had to go to Issa, he would help. He was the sensible child in the family after all. I needed to find him on his own and tell him everything – that was my only option and way out.

***

We hadn't even finished our big plate of sardines when Um Suleiman turned up. Zakaria looked startled when she towered over our table. He was still biting into a large fish as he looked up and tried to smile. I gave her a big hug and introduced her to my friend. He wiped his hands and offered to shake hers, but she refused.

'No, I am not conservative – your hands are just dirty. The smell of fish sticks to your body for a while; you'd better wipe your hands with a lemon.'

He relaxed into his seat and laughed.

'So, you are Zakaria Abu Qamar, son of Hussam?'

'How did you know?' he asked, as he squeezed lemon into his palms.

'I have lived in Jabalia Camp for a long time. I have known you since you were a kid. I even changed your nappy a couple of times. Your father is a good man, how is his health these days?'

'Good, thank you. Much better, after the pills the doctor prescribed.'

'Good, well, he might not feel better after he knows that you've been going around sticking your nose into other people's business. What brings you out here?'

I saw that Zakaria was becoming uncomfortable and felt the remarks were unfair.

'Um Suleiman, I asked Zakaria to bring me here. I went to his house to ask for his help.' I said quickly.

Zakaria looked as though he had fire around his eyes.

'Okay, well, his help is not needed anymore. He can leave whenever he wants to, I will sort out the bill.'

'No one is paying for my food,' he shouted. 'You are not my damn mother.' I felt awful about how awkward the situation had become.

'Um Suleiman, it is not that bad, Zakaria has been looking after me. Please don't get upset.'

She seemed to swallow whatever she was about to say. Zakaria got out fifty shekels from his pocket and placed them on the table.

'Let's go, Zahra,' he said to me sharply.

'Where to?' I asked, as Um Suleiman bit her tongue.

'Somewhere else, where we can talk properly.'

'I need to see Um Suleiman, I haven't seen her for ages.' I said, pretending I had known her for a long time.

'Well, maybe we can come back here after we've talked, I am sure she wouldn't mind waiting a bit.' He looked at her with suspicion. I could see he was trying to figure out whether her arrival was simply a coincidence. 'Zahra, don't listen to these people, don't trust them – they are not on your side. Listen, here's my number, call me If you ever need me. I am going to leave now.' He grabbed a wet wipe from the table, cleaned his hands and headed to the door.

'Wait,' I said, unsure why. 'I want you to stay a while.'

Zakaria paused and leant against the doorframe.

'It's better if he continues on his way,' Um Suleiman interjected. 'Listen to me, Zahra, this man is not trustworthy, you will soon realise and regret going to see him.'

I was becoming baffled, not knowing who to trust anymore. Why would Um Suleiman have so much aggression towards Zakaria? He hadn't done anything to her. She dragged me to a corner and whispered in my ear.

'This man doesn't have a good reputation in Jabalia Camp, everyone knows he is a big womaniser and a drunk. The police gave him a warning last time – they said if they ever caught him drunk again, they would arrest him for life.'

A drunk in Jabalia Camp! What an entertaining thought, it almost made me chuckle. I would've liked to see Zakaria walking around out of his mind while Israel bombed us left, right and centre. I wondered what he would have shouted back at the jets!

'No one trusts him in the Camp, why should you? Anyway, you need to go and see Nouman, he is still waiting for you.'

'I will, Um Suleiman, let's go together – but first let me have a private word with Zakaria.'

I walked over to him and he smiled as if victorious.

Chapter 13

'I need to trust someone, Zakaria. For God's sake, I need to know that you are on my side.' I spoke to him as if we'd been friends for a long time, but at that moment I just needed to hang onto any hope I could find. I was on my own, tangling myself deeper and deeper in trouble.

'You have my word, Zahra, that's the best that I can offer right now. Oh, and all the years of genuinely fancying you, which have . . . erm . . . never disappeared.' He looked away from me, blushing.

'Good, I need to you to go to someone for me. Her name is Wafa El Astal, she lives in Khan Younis. She is a friend of mine. We are . . . well, were very close when we were studying at university.'

He was staring at me like a little kid waiting to be given a task that would make him feel like a grown up. His eyes were round and his body tense, awaiting further instructions, but the truth was that I didn't know why I wanted him to go to Wafa. Maybe I felt I had no ally anymore, and maybe having someone else knowing what was going on would be useful.

'Tell her everything that has happened – our meeting with Abu Eyyad and all the strange things we've gone through today. But most importantly, give her this key to my apartment and ask her to wait for me there.'

Without hesitation, Zakaria took the key from me and headed off without looking at Um Suleiman. His tall, well-built body became a dark silhouette in the now blazing sun. As he walked away, I started to wonder how to find my brother Issa. He was my only hope.

Um Suleiman watched Zakaria disappear too, before she turned to me and nodded, ushering me out of the restaurant.

I followed her in silence. She seemed to be on a mission to get me to Nouman. After about a fifteen-minute walk, we turned left and climbed a few hilly roads until we arrived at the Twam Junction to wait for a taxi. We found one quickly, which took us to the eye hospital in El Nasser area, where we changed taxis and jumped into another one to El Saha in Gaza City.

Um Suleiman only talked to me when we got in the second taxi, which sped through El Nasser Street, all the way down to Rashad El Shawwa Centre, then turned left towards Omar El Mukhtar Street. The smell of the fresh, salty air quickly disappeared, to be replaced by fumes coming from the traffic in the city centre. I thought it was a longer route to take; the driver could have done a U-turn and gone down towards Jalaa Street, right towards El Saraya and then left again to El Saha in Gaza City. But I wasn't in any hurry.

My initial excitement to see Nouman had subsided. I wasn't sure why – he hadn't done anything wrong. Maybe it was the fact that he now knew a lot about my life; in fact, he knew more than I did.

'Why did you go to see that loser?' Um Suleiman asked sharply.

'You don't like him, do you?' I wasn't really asking, more making a statement.

'No, of course not, no one does. He has a bad reputation in the Camp for being a womaniser, a drunk and a drug addict. I think these are enough reasons not to like him. What I don't understand is why a woman like you would go to visit him at home.'

'That's no one's business,' I responded sharply.

'Don't you see? He will damage your reputation in the Camp, many people will start to talk about you and, as always, the subject will become the woman rather than the man.'

'I don't have a reputation to worry about anyway, it is damaged already.'

'You shouldn't say that, trust me, you don't want to be associated with this person.'

We both fell silent. I didn't want any more lectures from a woman I hardly knew. But for some reason, I trusted her, maybe because Mother was a little absent in all of this. Um Suleiman knew how to demand trust and win it easily from people. The way she talked to the driver so smoothly with a commanding voice gave her the aura of a woman in charge, not afraid of being around men. She spoke to me like a mother, to the driver like a fellow driver, to Zakaria like his school bully. She knew how to position herself and to speak to people as their equal.

We got to El Saha and started walking towards the big white municipality building. The walls stood tall, and the two main gates, with the arches built of Jerusalem stones, were very clean. I saw a few people walking across the small square towards the main entrance, which had two staircases, one at either side, leading up to a big wooden gate, which was ajar. To my surprise, we didn't go through the main gate, but Um Suleiman carried on to the side of the main wall and started going down El Wihda Street towards Fras Market. The side wall was peppered with small metal arches that formed stalls for a mini market. The stalls were crammed full of antiques, silverware and political memorabilia. There were maps of Palestine carved on pieces of olive wood; refugee symbol Handala on keychains and necklaces; silver long keys to represent the right of return; the ubiquitous cheap golden replicas of the Dome of Rock. They were all laid out on shelves fixed to the wall. There were shutters at either side which the stall owners used when they were closed for business. We walked down until we reached a stall where the shutters were slapped tightly together.

Um Suleiman stopped in the middle of the busy pavement, outside the closed stall. She looked around for a bit, then knocked three times on the metal shutters. For some reason, the owners on both sides of the stall didn't seem to react – as if nothing had happened. I looked around to see if anyone was watching. A couple of passers-by glanced towards me but didn't look very interested. It was like business as usual for them. Then the shutters opened, and someone wearing a balaclava peered out and ushered us in.

We followed the masked man into a very dark tunnel, big enough for us to walk through. He was walking quickly, carrying a lantern containing a small candle. We continued until we got to a door. The man knocked and Nouman's voice came ringing through my ears.

'Come in! Zahra, welcome. I am so relieved you are here.' He was not looking at me but examining a paper in his hand.

The room was almost bare. There was a table in the middle with two chairs on opposite sides. There was also an old brown sofa at the side, and a pile of books on the floor in the corner, but that was it, nothing else.

'What is this Nouman? Some secret interrogation room? What am I doing here?'

'It is for your safety.'

'What safety? Why am I in danger?'

'We will talk in a minute, first give all your belongings to Um Suleiman, she will look after them for you – especially any mobile phone you may have.'

'What? Why?'

'Just do as I say.'

'No!' I shouted, and my voice rang in the empty room. The masked man started to approach me.

'Don't let me make him do it, Zahra. You have to, and you need to trust me.' Nouman spoke with hesitation.

'Make him? Who the fuck is he anyway? Are you trying to scare me? I can't believe I trusted you! Why are you doing this to me?'

Um Suleiman started walking towards me, and in that

moment I felt lonely again, cursing myself for being so stupid and getting myself into this situation. Why did I not listen to Jamil and forget about the whole thing? Why did I have to cause trouble? I didn't know what to think or feel; I just started emptying my pockets as she came closer to me.

She stared at me for a while before taking my wallet, my phone and even my wedding ring. I pulled it out of my pocket and paused, looking at it, before handing everything over. For some crazy reason, I felt like I was giving it back to Ammar, as if I were divorcing him. I wished he'd been the one to receive it. I wished he was there so I could shout at him and ask why the fuck he'd lived a double life, why he had never told me anything about those secret missions of his. My brother and husband used to do stuff together; they used to go to Abu Eyyad's farm and hang out. How did I not know about all of this?

At that moment, I started to care less about Ammar and think more about the stupid person I was. Surrounded by two men and a woman – who now looked fiercer than both men – I felt small, insignificant and not worthy of knowing the truth.

'Take a seat, Zahra.' Nouman began speaking.

'Have they invented an electric sofa now? The chair is not good enough?' I said walking towards it without looking at him. I heard Nouman laughing loudly.

'You do make me laugh, Zahra.'

'Good, I am glad to be of service,' I snapped, still not looking at him.

'Listen to me carefully. You are not being arrested, interrogated, kidnapped or any of the above. You are free to go right now if you wish, but listen to me first, and if you still decide to leave, then feel free. But whatever happens, you have to promise not to tell anyone about this place, whether you decide to leave now or when the whole thing is over. This is a secret place. Many people, great people, have used it as a hiding place. Imad Aqil lived here for six months.'

'How can it be that secret if we came directly from the street and every single stall seller saw us climb up here?' I said quickly.

'Secrets are kept by spreading other rumours. This is the power of this place and the people around. These stall sellers won't say a word. It is a tradition that has been passed down for generations. They will sniff around and find out if word has spread. Gaza is small, we can deal with it then or just spread another story.'

'You seem confident!'

'Indeed, I am. Now listen to me carefully, I am getting closer to figuring out who killed your husband.'

I collapsed on the sofa. There was a pain in my stomach and I felt like throwing up for the second time that day. My head was spinning. I wanted to cry but I couldn't. I thought that it would relieve me to let my tears flow, but nothing came out. I had dried up completely.

'Are you okay, Zahra?' Um Suleiman asked.

'Yes.' I didn't want her to come any closer; I felt insulted by how formal she was being, even though I didn't know her very well.

'Sorry,' I managed to say, 'I guess the relief of knowing that I am not deluded is overwhelming. Thank you, Mr. Nouman.'

'I thought we agreed not to call me Mr. Nouman.'

'Yes, sorry.'

'Now, as I was saying, I believe I am getting closer to knowing who killed your husband. What I am lacking is the evidence, but I am working on that at the moment. In the meantime, your life is in danger. The killer is out there and has got word that I have been digging for information. This is why you were followed the other day, and why someone broke into your family home in Jabalia Camp. They wanted to know what evidence you had so far. I am afraid they might decide that the best course of action is to get rid of you. This is why you are here. It is better not to use technology, hence why we are taking your mobile and belongings. I don't know who the killer is connected to and what they can and can't do. so it's better not to use your personal phone; Um Suleiman will assist you in getting in and out of this place, but will not accompany you everywhere. We don't want to tailgate you or anything like that; we just want to ensure your safety and the secrecy of this place.'

'How would I communicate with Um Suleiman if I don't have a mobile phone?'

'The good old fashion way,' Nouman said quickly. 'You call her on the landline using a public phone box.'

I looked at her. She was smiling this time, perhaps apologising for her roughness earlier. I wondered why she was so involved, and why it wasn't her husband there instead, as it was he who was more involved with the resistance.

'Now,' Nouman continued, 'will you stay and trust me?'

The silence which followed was very painful. I couldn't speak for a few long seconds. I was bewildered and unsure what to say. Of course, I didn't trust him anymore – no woman would trust a man who brought her to some secret dungeon and pretended it was for her safety. I looked at him, pleading with my eyes, asking him to be truthful and give me a sign that he was being straight with me. His face was neutral, it showed no emotions.

'Okay,' I said, barely audible, 'I have no other choice, do I?'

'You do Zahra, we all do,' he said, with a slight hint of a smile that was neither reassuring nor scary.

'Okay, I've got to go out now, and Um Suleiman needs to go home to her husband and family. I will be back later.'

'Wait, what? So I am staying in this room with this ninja guy. What is your name, man?'

'I am afraid he can't tell you his name – he is the guardian of this place. You will be in safe hands, and you'll be shown where the toilet is when you need it.' Nouman picked up my things from the table and prepared to leave.

'I put some books in the corner for you. There is some Shakespeare stuff that I don't understand, and another – a woman called Jane Eyerrr or something. Oh and I picked some Palestinian novels too: *Men in the Sun* by Ghassan Kanafani and *The Pessoptimist* by Emil Habebi, in case you fancied reading something in Arabic. I was looking for Sahar Khalifeh's *Wild Thornes* but I couldn't find it. Maybe tomorrow, *inshallah*.'

'Does this man talk?' I looked at the masked man in the corner.

'Yes I do,' he responded quickly and sharply, 'but I won't tell you my name, I never tell anybody.'

'Okay,' Nouman said, 'I will see you two later then. Shall we go, Um Suleiman?'

And with that, they were gone, the same way I came in. The room looked even emptier then. The light bulb hanging in the middle started to flicker, then went dimmer. Or maybe I imagined it – my brain wasn't working properly.

'Shall we have a bet?' I said to the masked man.

'About what?' His voice was very deep.

'That by the end of this – if it ever does end – you will have told me your name?'

'Okay. What is the bet?'

'Three hundred shekels,' I said.

'Can you afford this?' he asked sarcastically.

'Of course. My husband and I worked full time and never had children, so I can take a gamble.'

'You are on; sorry to take your money.'

'We will see about that,' I laughed.

***

Hours passed, and there was no sign of Nouman. I couldn't tell what time it was. My masked companion said only a few words. He occupied himself with reading a pocket size copy of the Quran. I went to the corner where Nouman had left the books and looked through them. To my surprise, I found one of my favourite books in English. *His Dark Materials* by Philip Pullman. The entire series was lying there. I picked up *The Northern Lights* and touched it with my hand. I could not believe my luck. On the first page, the stamp of the British Council's library had almost faded – it was dated 19th September 2009. I started reading, travelling back in time to when Ammar and I had talked about the books. I was a big fan of fantasy writing. Ammar was a bit of a snob when it came to anything to do with popular culture, but to my mind, considering the prison we lived in, any fantasy was more than welcome. I wanted to know that there was a world beyond the one that Israel confined us in.

Ammar, on the other hand, wanted to immerse himself in great literary geniuses. He read Graham Swift, Ian McEwan and the like. He was a fan of Irish literature, he loved Yeats and Heaney and always thought there was a similarity between what they talked about and the Palestinian cause.

'If only they lived here, they would have told the world about our plight so eloquently,' he would say, as if he were sending a message to them telepathically, so they could rise from their deathbeds to be here in this godforsaken prison called Gaza.

'But we have Mahmoud Darwish, Sameeh El Qassim and many others who say eloquent things – it is the world that doesn't want to listen. I bet if your Irish heroes were living here no one would have heard about them, just the same as they don't know about our writers.'

He challenged me to mention any Palestinian writer who had ever attempted anything like *Ulysses* or any work by the great James Joyce. But how could anyone write about a quirky

Mr. Bloom in Gaza? He would most likely have either been shot by the Israelis in the first instance, or excommunicated and banished by this society. I often made the point to Ammar that we produced the best literature in the Arab World; an inherited tradition of storytelling that continued to be at the heart of all our literary works. I reminded him of his own great cousin, Muin Bseiso, who wrote wonderful poetry which Palestinians would cherish forever.

I knew that deep inside, Ammar loved fantasy books too, because he went to great lengths to discuss them with me, even if just to tell me that his taste in books was better. He would listen to me carefully and ask the sort of questions only an intrigued person would. He would never admit it though. English Literature students could be arrogant. They liked to believe they had such an extraordinary mental capacity that only great philosophical works could fulfil them. Everything else was just a waste of mental energy that could be invested in the attempt to solve world problems and the eternal question of existence. Those students also tended to be male.

I started reading, imagining little Lyra, the gypsies, the ship, armoured polar bears, hot air balloons and demons. Everyone in the book had their own demon – their subconscious in the form of a creature. It reflected their personality, from a monkey to a tiger to a snake. I looked around the room and saw my masked man still reading his holy book. I wondered whether he was in fact my own demon – my subconscious manifesting itself in the form of this masked man.

'Are you Hamas?' I asked him, as if asking myself. I wanted to have a reaffirming answer that I wasn't.

'No,' he said, to my relief.

'Why are you covering your face then?'

'What has that got to do with anything? Balaclavas aren't exclusive to Hamas. I just don't want people to know who I am.'

'Oh, the guardian of this place and all that,' I said sarcastically, which he didn't appreciate.

'My daughter, listen to me! We don't do this because we want to, because we think it is great to cover our faces and sit in a sunless, airless room. But this place is wounded by the occupation, by constant occupiers who always want a piece of this country. I don't know why, but they want it. They all want to destroy our spirit, we the people who have lived here for centuries. They want the land but don't want us. This is why we have to resist, hide, run, fight and do all of that. It's the natural reaction to what they do to us.'

There was something in his voice which made me realise he truly believed every word he was saying. I didn't believe all of it, but it wasn't my place to argue with a guy who spent most of his time in hiding. He clearly believed it was important.

'Does Hamas know about this place?'

'No . . . er . . . well some members do.'

I went back to my book, back to reading about parallel universes – just like where I was in a way. I wanted to read more. I wanted to explore the possibility of a multiverse in Gaza. Maybe if I started digging into this dungeon I would eventually get somewhere – a paradise – or maybe I would reach the heart of darkness and pluck it out.

I found myself muttering, in a low voice, John Milton's famous words from *Paradise Lost*:

> *Into this wilde Abyss,*
> *The Womb of nature and perhaps her Grave,*
> *Of neither Sea, nor Shore, nor Air, nor Fire,*
> *But all these in their pregnant causes mixt,*
> *Confus'dly, and which thus must ever fight.*

'Nouman told me some people believe there is a treasure hidden in the walls of this building, from the time of Sultan

Abdulhameed. Is this true?'

The masked man closed his Quran and looked at me. I could swear he was smiling underneath the mask. His eyes looked very kind, and he stared at me for a few seconds before answering. He got up, went to the other side of the room and crouched down in the corner, fixing his eyes on a small brick beside a pillar.

'A lot of people have tried to find it, some have left messages here. Come and have a read!'

I walked over, expecting to read some coded treasure hunt message, but when I got there, only a few words of despair were left on the wall. "He who attempts to find the treasure will never find happiness" and, written with a more philosophical approach, "To find the treasure, you must first cleanse yourself from all evil thoughts".

'How about we go looking for it together and we can split the gold?' I heard him laugh for the first time; he was really amused.

'What makes you think that if I knew where the treasure was I would go looking for it with you, then split it? Why not just find it by myself? I am always here anyway.' He continued to laugh.

I smiled and headed back to my sofa. On the way back, I saw a copy of Shakespeare's *Richard II*, lying on its own near the big pile of books. I stopped and bent down to pick it up. It reminded me of Ammar, nostalgia for the good old days at El Azhar University came rushing over me, reading English Literature and dreaming of a world far away. Our professors back then were pompous pricks who all got their PhDs in the United States. They loved putting on their best American accent, trying to differentiate themselves from us locals, who spoke English with a heavy Arabic accent tinged with local Gazan pronunciation. A girl in our class was ridiculed for the way she pronounced the word 'kerfuffle'. "It is not falafel," the teacher joked, and the whole class burst into wild laughter.

I stood up again and kicked *Richard II* with my foot. 'Die you fool,' I muttered under my breath, and it felt very satisfying.

***

I had been completely immersed in my reading for a long time. I looked around, and my masked man had disappeared. I was all alone in the room, lying on the sofa with my book. Nouman hadn't come back and I wasn't sure what time it was. I guessed it was about five hours since we left the beach, so it would have been 8 p.m. by then. I got up and started to search for the bathroom. I traced the walls with my fingers and saw some writing in Arabic.

"Whatever the jailer does to my body, my soul would always be intact immersed in your love, Palestine, like a piece of bread dipping into a bowl of olive oil. Imad Aqil". Another quote was by Yahya Ayyash: "Mother, I have no regrets about what I do except that I can't see you as much as I want. Omi, I miss you".

A strange feeling crept over me as I read those words of legendary resistance fighters, those who gave the Israeli soldiers a hard time, those who had become heroes in our society. Stories were often told about their genius: about how many Israeli soldiers they killed while defending our people; bedtime tales of Imad Aqil dressing up as an Israeli soldier and going right to the heart of their base. I felt their spirit with me in the room; somehow I felt inadequate to be in such company. I had never been active in the resistance movement myself, and although I teased Ammar for not throwing stones at Israeli soldiers in the First Intifada, I realised that I too, had hardly done so. Yes, I went on demonstrations and shouted my head off, maybe threw a couple of rocks or three, but my heart had never really been in it.

But that revolutionary woman was growing inside me day after day: every time I ran home from school, trying to dodge Israeli teargas canisters in the First Intifada in 1987; each time I saw an old woman being humiliated by a blonde teenage soldier with sunglasses on, tossing the woman aside and pulling her headscarf off her head. The revolutionary woman inside me became more dominant when Israeli F16s started bombing us during the Second Intifada in 2000, when I watched women striking outside the Red Cross compound in Gaza City, demanding the release of their family members from Israeli prisons. I cried silently, cursed our lives, and like the rest of my people I condemned the silence of the world we lived in, became angry with myself and my people. I had thoughts about armed resistance but I never did anything about it, and instead I ended up marrying the most passive man imaginable. Perhaps going to university was my way of resisting; perhaps wanting to live a normal life was like sticking my finger up in the face of occupation. Maybe being a successful woman in Gaza was, in itself, resistance; maybe changing people around me was my mission. I didn't know whether anyone would agree with me, but I knew I was never going to be in any history book.

Imad Aqil and Yehya Ayyash; who would have thought I would be in their company one day? Who would have thought the two men might be hovering over me trying to protect me as much as they tried to protect Palestine, the homeland? They belonged to a different era, to the time of the First Intifada: the time of stone throwing; the time of innocence and hope, when Palestinians thought they might have a state one day; when they all stood up as one and threw stones at soldiers to express their anger at the killing of civilians. These days, such acts elsewhere in the Arab world might be dubbed the 'Arab Spring', or perhaps some kind of revolution, but not for us Palestinians. Aqil and Ayyash were our hope, and remained so for a long time. Their ability to resist was remarkable. Their incredible and creative ways of making the soldiers despair were ingenious. I wanted to be like them, I wanted to be with them in that time of hopefulness. I found a marker pen on the floor and wrote underneath what they had written: "Palestine, I am like you; we are both betrayed by the people around us. Signed Zahra Tanani, 02 January 2016".

***

The door opened and my masked man reappeared carrying several black plastic bags.

'Where's Nouman?' I asked immediately.

'I thought he would be here by now. I just went out to get some food. Are you hungry?'

'Yes, but I need the toilet more than anything.'

'Come this way.' He led me through the red metal door, back into the tunnel. We walked a short way, then he opened another small door on the right-hand side of the tunnel which opened onto some stairs. I lowered my body, legs first, to get onto the stairs, and started descending backwards. At the bottom, there was another door opening into a tiny, stinky bathroom.

Back in the room, my demon emptied the plastic bags onto the table, laying out *shawarma*, olives, bread, olive oil, *mutabbal*, feta cheese, water, Fanta bottles and napkins.

'Are you going to eat?' I asked, although my question really was, 'Are you going to take your mask off?'

'Yes. I will go to the sofa, you stay at the table. I will face the other way – please don't try looking.'

'Why would I do that? It's not like you are Johnny Depp, is it?' He didn't seem to understand my reference, or maybe he just couldn't be bothered to reply. He went to the sofa and started what looked like a well-practiced routine of taking off his mask so he could eat.

I looked at this man covered in black and thought how wasted our youth was. Most of us in Gaza had to pay a heavy price for this occupation, whether hiding away, pretending it didn't exist – like my idiot husband – or facing it head on like Aqil and Ayyash. But I wasn't sure where I fitted into the whole thing. I was neither here nor there. All the people I knew had a strong reaction to occupation, one way or the other, but not me – I was somewhere in the middle.

As he started eating, I glanced back and stole a quick look at him, then started to shake. There was something about the way he was eating, his presence, the way he sat, and even the sound of chewing food, that made me realise my guard was no other than Mohammed El Deif, Mohammed the Guest. There was no doubt in my mind that he was the same person who the Israelis had attempted to assassinate over thirty times, the leader of the military wing of Hamas, the Qassam Brigades, the man whose identity had been hidden from everyone in Gaza and Palestine, who was believed to be from the West Bank and came to our Strip as a guest. The person who only appeared as a shadow on recorded video messages, the one who controlled the entire resistance against Israeli occupation forces, who had led many military operations against them. He was the most wanted man of all time, and had a heavy price over his head.

How could this be? Why did Nouman put me in such danger? If Israel knew he was here, they would bomb the entire building within moments. They broke a UN-brokered ceasefire within seconds on 4th August 2014 after receiving intelligence that El Deif was in a house in Sheikh Radwan area, visiting his sister. They killed the entire family and a hundred other people in Rafah without flinching.

I thought I was in the company of ghosts, of past great heroes like Ayyash and Aqil, but now realised I was dining with our national hero himself. The person about whom everyone tells stories, of how Israel had failed to capture him. The person a lot of people claim has defended us against Israeli aggression and reduced our casualties.

Yet I didn't want to be there, I didn't choose to be with him.

I looked away from him and wondered what was going to become of me, there was no way out of this now. No one would ever let me out of here. Of course, there wasn't any way for me to know for sure this person was Mohammed El Deif. Would he kill me if he knew I suspected that? The only thing I could think of was to keep silent, not to tell him my suspicions and to forget about my banter with him. But my curiosity was stronger than anything else. Wanting to be left in no doubt, I turned around for one more look, and at that moment he was staring back at me with no mask on at all. His eyes glowed in the small, dimly lit room. I turned my face away but it was too late, our eyes had met.

It was him. The image of young Mohammed El Deif's face, drawn by an artist on a leaflet dropped by Israeli planes, offering a million dollars for information about him, was now vivid in my mind. These leaflets became the joke at Jabalia Camp for a long time, we laughed at the stupidity of the Israeli army and the badly drawn cartoon-like face. There was a phone number at the bottom of the leaflet, so a few people decided to play tricks and call it non-stop, saying that El Deif had been sighted in Rafah, then in Jabalia and Khan Younis in the south of the Strip, and some people demanded the money because the leaflet didn't say what information the Israelis wanted. Within twenty-four hours the phone number wasn't working anymore, and in that time it had received over half a million calls. It was like a coordinated popular phone protest. Other people drew a similar cartoon picture of Netanyahu, the Israeli Prime Minister, offering a similar price for information about him, and pinned it everywhere in the Camp.

But now, seeing this face in real life, I could appreciate the similarity. It was him, no doubt. In fact, I admired the artist who'd made the initial image out of nothing but their imagination.

I heard him move his chair and stand up, he walked

closer to me while I still faced the other way, refusing to look back again. I heard a gun being cocked and waited for the sound of a bullet to rip through the air. Without thinking, I started reciting verses from the Quran, thinking that this was it, my death was just a few steps away.

Then just as he reached my side, I stood up and turned around to face him. He was pointing his gun towards me, and his mask was back in place.

'You don't need to bother with your mask anymore, I know who you are.'

He placed his finger on the trigger.

'I know you could shoot me and no one would care, I am finished anyway. No one knows I am here, already tangled in disgrace, my family won't care about me, and of course the Qassam Brigades will just throw my body to some wild dogs to rip apart.'

He took his mask off. I was shocked. He was a beautiful man.

'Go on, do it. I've had enough anyway.' I closed my eyes and waited. But nothing happened, he didn't pull the trigger. I opened my eyes again and saw him staring at me in silence.

'Please do it, put me out of my misery.' But there was still no response. Instead, he lowered his gun, un-cocked it and took all the bullets out as he returned to his seat. He put his mask on again, picked up a copy of the Quran and started reading in a loud voice.

I crouched down in my spot and began to cry tears of relief. When you get close to death, the mind starts playing tricks. It blocks all emotion, builds up a wall of steel around itself to ease the pain of the imminent loss of life. Then when death doesn't happen, and you survive, that wall comes crashing down like a set of dominoes. You can almost hear it, and the only thing you can do is weep.

Chapter 14

The next morning, there was still no sign of Nouman. Um Suleiman turned up at midday, bringing a nightdress and some underwear, as well as a toothbrush, which I desperately needed. She hadn't heard anything from Nouman either; her face looked puffy and she turned away when I asked her about him.

'Have you tried calling him?' I asked.

'No, Nouman will be back soon. I don't want to make things more difficult for him.'

She emptied all the bags on the sofa and handed me the toothbrush.

'Your breath stinks,' she said, with a slight hint of a smile.

'Thanks, yes, I was really worried about that. Luckily, my companion has a mask on his face, so I am assuming he can't smell much.'

'I can,' he responded, his voice hoarse, as though he hadn't slept all night.

Um Suleiman saw me blush and finally smiled properly.

'When do you think he will be back?'

'I don't know, Zahra, I wish I could tell you that.'

***

A whole day passed and there was still no sign of my detective. What had happened to him? Was this what he wanted? To trap me there in a prison? Lots of thoughts stormed my head; I felt paranoid and panicky. I wanted to get out of there as soon as possible. He had tricked me into this.

I shouted at Mohammed and shook him violently.

'I'm sorry, there's nothing I can do,' he kept repeating.

163

'I need to get out of here. Call Um Suleiman.'

He did, and she came within an hour, looking cross with me.

'I need to get out of here, I am dying. Where's Nouman?'

'I don't know,' she said, looking away to hide her obvious concern. 'Come, let's go out for a while.'

'I need to speak to my family, they must be worried about me right now! I also need to go home to check on the flat.'

'I don't think that's a good idea, Zahra. You can call your family from a public phone booth but I wouldn't advise going back to the flat. We need to check this with Nouman, who I am sure wouldn't agree.'

'What, is he my guardian now?' I was very annoyed by the way she spoke to me, as though I were a small child waiting for a parent's permission.

We went through the tunnel, back to the main trap door. Um Suleiman knocked lightly and someone opened it up. We jumped out onto the street, covered in dust. The man in the makeshift shop next door pretended not to see us and carried on chatting to a woman. They were discussing the price of cigarettes and the high tax Hamas had imposed on people.

The sunlight almost blinded me. People looked like shadows; I couldn't see properly, rubbing my eyelids until they started to burn. We walked up towards El Saha, past the big arches of the municipality building. I was struggling to keep up with Um Suleiman. My muscles were numb, I hadn't used them for a couple of days.

My mother's voice came very softly on the phone. I could hear the tears filling her throat. She wanted me to go home. She told me how much she missed me and how sorry she was for being so sharp when we met near Zakaria's house. She begged me to come home so we could talk things through. I could hear Jamil and Issa in the background, arguing, then the voices started getting louder and Jamil grabbed the receiver.

'Come home immediately!' he shouted.

I was silent, not knowing what to say. He had this threatening manner which made me shiver. I looked at Um Suleiman who seemed to understand. She shook her head disapprovingly.

'Give me Mum back, please! I don't want to talk to you.'

He started shouting even more, swearing he would kill me if he got hold of me. Just like he killed my husband, I thought. Why did he hate me so much? Why was he determined to ruin any hope left in me? We fought a lot when we were kids, the same way as any siblings in the world, over toys, clothes, food. He was always the first to run to Mother and complain about me. He wouldn't dare speak to Father because he knew Dad was always on my side. Oh, how I missed that beautiful man, I wished he was here right now.

Jamil came home from school once with his clothes all dirty. I was outside our house playing with the girls on the street. I asked him what had happened, but he refused to speak to me. My friends and I laughed and carried on playing, but then I heard Mum's voice shouting from inside the house. I ran inside to find her furious with me. He had told her I'd thrown dirt on him just before he entered the house. I swore on my life I hadn't, and asked Mother to check my story with the girls outside, but she refused and gave me a bad beating.

Later, Jamil came to my room with a grin on his face. I couldn't look at him. I didn't understand why he had done that or what had happened to him in the first place. We didn't speak for a whole week afterwards. Father noticed and asked us to tell him what had happened. When I told him everything, he was furious with Jamil and sent him to his room to stay there until he told the truth. He threatened to suspend his pocket money and not allow him to go to school. Jamil came out of his room, looking sheepish. He confessed he had made it up, but only because I had laughed at him, and he'd wanted to teach me a lesson. Mother was embarrassed too and apologised to me.

Issa took the receiver from my younger brother and spoke to me calmly and softly.

'Zahra, listen to me carefully. I don't know what has happened but whatever it is we can work it out.' He was pleading with me to listen. 'I am your older brother and want the best for you. If Father was here, I wouldn't be talking about it, but it is my responsibility to keep the family together. Please, don't make it harder for me!'

'You don't understand, Issa,' I said quickly.

'Try me, please.' His voice was strained, and it was clear he was losing hope that I would listen to him.

'It's complicated, Issa. Hopefully, one day, I will able to explain. But I have learned a great deal of stuff that I was oblivious to before. Things that would shock you too.'

'I am all ears,' he said.

'Not now, I need to see you. Can you meet me in the vegetable market near El Saha please? Has Zakaria Abu Qamar come asking for me?'

Um Suleiman was getting impatient, telling me to hurry up as I fed the phone more coins to carry on with the call.

'Who? Zakaria, no. Why? Okay, I will meet you in the market. See you there at 2 p.m.'

I hung up while Mother was still talking in the background, shouting at me to come home. I turned to Um Suleiman, who started walking towards Shujaia. I wasn't sure where she was heading. We continued walking past El Ahli Hospital and crossed to the other side, close to the old Omari Mosque. We went through the covered gold market first, then descended a few steps of the mosque. The big arches stood as beautiful as they had always done since the Umayyad period. Um Suleiman headed for the big wooden door and knocked on it three times. An old man wearing a thick grey *jellabiya* opened the door and invited us in.

'This is going to be your second hiding place, Zahra. We will use both alternately depending how safe things are. You are free to go wherever you like now, but please remember to let me know when you are coming back and I will advise which place to meet at. There's no immediate danger to your life now, but I would rather you didn't go back home or attempt to stay at your family's. Try to remain unnoticed when you move around.'

There was something about her air of authority, and I felt obliged to follow her instructions, even if I couldn't trust her completely. She spoke to the man for a while and then headed for the door, handing me some cash and her mobile number on a piece of paper. She had thought this through, because her number had been saved on my phone which I didn't have anymore.

'Um Suleiman!' She turned around. 'Thank you for everything.'

She didn't respond, but carried on walking. I followed her onto the street, but she was gone already. I saw the back of her white headscarf and started to run after her, but she turned, disappeared into the alleyways and was gone. A few children stopped their football game and asked me if they could help with anything.

Once again, I was back on the street roaming around, but this time unsure what I was looking for. Previously, I had been looking for a detective. But now, I had one who seemed to have disappeared. What was I looking for this time? My masked man must have asked for my removal from the other place. I didn't know why, but they probably thought it was best for me not to spend any more time with him. I felt that although I was relatively free to go where I wanted, I was being tracked – maybe I was still useful to Mohammed? Perhaps he didn't kill me the night before for that reason.

The only thing I could think of was to take a taxi to Khan Younis in the south, to track down Zakaria and Wafa. I could go to her house. I walked back to El Ahli hospital and jumped in a taxi heading to Khan Younis. The driver was in no rush, he wanted to fill his seven-seater, orange Mercedes cab with passengers before he set off. I offered to pay for the missing passenger. The taxi sped down to the Shujaia junction, past the YMCA and the Baptist School, then turned right onto Salah El Din Road, which ran all the way through the Gaza Strip, from north to south.

I had to pinch my nose when we crossed over Wadi Gaza because of the smell of sewage. What was once a beautiful river had become a dumping ground, mainly from bordering Israeli settlements. But then, the smell quickly changed to pine trees mixed with a strong hint of the olive groves nearby. I could see the orange trees were laden with fruit; it was the season when everything was ripening.

We passed the Nitsareem Junction, named after an infamous Israeli settlement, which had been on that site before being taken down in 2005.

The drive to Khan Younis main junction took about forty-five minutes. When I asked the driver where my seatbelt was, trying hard to hide my fear of his crazy Formula One driving, he looked at me in the rear-view mirror and told me they sold them to tunnel traders. Then he turned right off the road, went through the main high street near Nasser Hospital and turned right again just near the Sports Club.

Wafa's flat was in a relatively modern building near Mashrou Amer. It looked more rundown than the last time I had visited, a long time ago. I stood outside and thought about what I was going to say to her. So much had happened since we last spoke, I wouldn't know where to start. Her flat was on the fourth floor. There was no sign of life and, by the look of it, no electricity. I was breathless by the time I got to her door. I knocked furiously but there was no answer. I sat on the steps to have a few minutes rest when the door next to her flat opened. To my complete shock, Masked Mohammed came out.

'They are not here,' he said 'The police took them this

morning. A man came in first and then several policemen took her away.'

'Where to? How the hell did you get here?' I said quickly, but then I realised it must have sounded like a stupid question to him. After all, this was the man who could move like a shadow, who had avoided the Israeli Mossad, one of the most advanced intelligence services in the world, for over thirty years.

'Is this why you didn't kill me? Because you knew I would lead you here?' He didn't respond.

I sat back down on the steps, thinking I had made a terrible mistake, that I'd put my friend and her family in danger.

'Did you say the police took her and her husband?' I was cursing myself for getting more people involved in my troubles.

'Her husband, Mahmoud El Astal? No, of course not, he is too powerful to be arrested like that. He knows practically everyone in the government. I wouldn't imagine a few policemen could come to his house and arrest him. This is his second home, by the way; he has a massive villa on the beach, near El Aqsa University. You could probably go there and check, but I wouldn't advise it. He has many security guards and they will ask a lot of questions.'

'Wait, what? He has a second house? He's too powerful? What are you talking about? Are you sure it is the same guy, Wafa's husband?' I asked eagerly, hoping there was some kind of mistake.

'Yes, I am talking about the same guy, of course. Wafa's husband. He has two wives. This is his second home.'

I thought nothing could surprise me anymore, but this was shocking. How had Wafa never mentioned she was the second wife? I thought we swore not to end up in this position ever. And why had she never told me that her husband was well connected with the government? She mentioned he worked as an IT manager at the Ministry of Transportation. She didn't mention he was some big shot in Hamas or its stupid government. She said that he was conservative, but that was it. I met him a couple of times in Gaza City when Wafa and I bumped into each other – he didn't look that important.

I collapsed on the staircase, feeling shaky with all this new information.

'Would you like to come in?' Mohammed asked

'No, thank you. Can I have a glass of water please?'

I wasn't thirsty, but I wanted him to disappear for a while. I wanted to be alone for a few moments. Not only did I not know my own husband, but it seemed that I didn't know my friends either. Mohammed El Deif was quick and came back in a few seconds. He saw my tears running like a broken tap. I needed to find Nouman. I wanted to understand what had been happening – people around me were disappearing and I had no idea why.

'Mohammed, why are you doing this? Why are you here?' I asked sharply.

He took his mask off, and he was smiling. 'I am not doing anything, you are.' His smile became wider. 'You know, I have lived my life in resistance, fighting for our people's right to exist and live in peace. Then almost a decade ago Hamas took over Gaza, an act of self-defence and survival as the Fatah party prepared to get rid of us all. I ordered the takeover. I thought it would be temporary, to protect ourselves and to ensure the survival of the resistance. But power corrupts, and a few people – people I am ashamed to call members of my party – became involved in illegal stuff. We are getting closer now.'

'What is going to become of me and my family?' I interrupted.

'I don't know, I can't promise anything. We are all for Palestine, that's what matters.'

'Can you do me a favour, please?' I pleaded, while looking at his beautiful face. 'Please keep my family out of this.'

'If I were you,' Mohammed replied, 'I would try to get into your brother's room and search for clues, go deeper into his world without him knowing. If he could hide the fact he spoke to your husband moments before he was killed, he could surely hide many other things. The question is what and where? I would start in his bedroom; that would be my suggestion.'

How had I not already thought of doing that? And why had Nouman not done it? But regardless, I suddenly felt as though I had something to do. I had a purpose. I could still make a difference. Though the reality of how difficult it would be hit me straight away, as our house was very crowded all the time. My two brothers' wives hardly left the house except for shopping in the market, and even then there were always kids in the house who would report back to Jamil and Issa. They would tell them I had been in the house, especially if I went in his bedroom.

'If I were you, I would also wear sunglasses and a boring black jilbab, so I was less recognisable on the street,' Mohammed said.

'Wow, years of hiding have surely taught you a trick or two' I said sarcastically. I looked at my loose headscarf and tight jeans and realised that in the process of being consumed by the search for my husband's killer, I had completely ignored all our social norms. Of course I never liked them, or conformed to them, but I was always afraid to take too many risks. I had also been absent from my flat and family house for a few days now, and surely there would be some sort of rumour going around about what happened to me. Um Shihada surely would be spreading word that I had been arrested due to my prostitution business.

***

My sunglasses looked a little incongruous with the boring black *jilbab*. The shopkeeper was surprised to see my transformation. He took the money from me and asked if I wanted black gloves to go with it. I declined.

I left the shop and phoned my home. Issa answered, and started shouting at me as soon as he heard my voice.

'Let's meet now, please,' I pleaded, but he wanted me to come home to Jabalia Camp.

'No, please let's meet in Gaza City, I can't go to the Camp.'

After I threatened to hang up and never phone again, Issa eventually agreed to meet me in El Saha Square.

I got into a cab whose driver kept staring at me in the rear-view mirror. Could he see the anxious look in my eyes beneath the glasses? I wasn't sure whether I was breathing loudly or not, so I tried to breathe slowly and make sure not to show any sign of nerves.

Issa was buying a large sack of tomatoes from a stall holder. I walked towards, him then stopped. What if he had informed Jamil? Would there be anyone around to force me to go home? So I decided to watch him for a while to see if he spoke to anyone else. My new young friend had given me a perfect idea when suggesting I go around in disguise. How had I not thought of this? It was paying off right then. I walked past Issa three times without him recognising me. I was just like any other woman in a long black dress, headscarf and dark sunglasses. Most women dressed like that in Gaza. I walked up and down to make sure he was not with anyone, and just as he started strolling towards El Saha main square I tapped him on the shoulder and told him who I was. He was in shock.

'What have you done to yourself? Why are you covered like that?' he almost shouted at me.

'Well, Jamil always found my dress sense inappropriate,

so I decided to change it just for him.' My brother was silent.

'Brother, I need to talk to you. Let's find somewhere, please!'

'Lead the way,' he said. 'You are the city girl, even though you look ridiculous in this outfit.'

We started walking back towards El Saha. There was a *dabke* dance group in the main square near the Phoenix Lower Jaw Statue. We stopped to watch for a while. There were about a dozen dancers, both girls and boys. They all held hands on that sunny day and danced their hearts out, with the music blasting like it was some sort of festival. They were dressed up in beautiful, traditional Palestinian costumes. The girls wore white dresses with handmade embroidery running through the top and bottom. The men were in long, stripy white and grey *qumbaz*, which were used by the farmers in the old days to protect them from the sun. The male dancers tucked them up to their waists to give them more freedom to jump and twirl. I found myself clapping to the sound of *dalouna* music and putting my hand close to my mouth so I could ululate, but then I remembered my stupid face mask and stopped.

'Jamil killed my husband,' I said to Issa, without even looking at him.

'What the hell? What are you talking about, Zahra? And why don't we go somewhere where no one can hear us.' Issa grabbed my hand and started dragging me away, but I pulled him back.

'I think it is perfect here, everyone is happy watching the dancers. No one will care much about us or my misery. The detective has been following all leads. We found a phone in my flat that Ammar used secretly. He made a phone call to Jamil only an hour and a half before he was killed.'

'What? Why? They didn't like each other. But . . . wait, I am confused, are you saying your brother killed your husband and your evidence is just a phone call?' Issa was pressing hard on my hand now. It hurt so much that I cried out. A woman in the crowd turned her head towards us and stared for a moment.

'No, there's more. They used to meet and do stuff all the time. They had some private matters they used to attend to together. There's a farmer in the El Soudania area who saw them together all the time, and what's worse, he saw them with Israelis, people coming out from the fence to meet them and talk to them. They were talking and doing some sort of business. They loaded boxes on donkey carts and mini trucks.'

'Zahra, stop this right now. If your detective is sure that Jamil killed Ammar, then why hasn't he arrested him yet? Jamil couldn't have had any dealings with the Israelis. Your brother is Hamas. Have you not realised that?'

'What?!' I was in total shock. 'What did you just say?'

'Yes, your brother is in the Qassam Brigades. He has been part of them for a long time now. He got in with them after he got married, because of his father-in-law, your Uncle Emad, the blacksmith. The one whose workshop was bombed several times under the pretext they were manufacturing weapons for the resistance. That was bullshit, of course, your uncle has never been involved in that kind of thing but, as a result, your brother Jamil joined the resistance. Why do you think he disappears every time there's a war on Gaza?'

'Oh . . . I just thought he was scared!' I said sheepishly. And I suddenly understood why Mohammed wanted me to go into my brother's room. They can't do it themselves, because Jamil is one of their own. They didn't want to make a scene and search their own members. Hamas was all about their image after all.

'No, your brother is never scared. That is his bloody problem, he's too brave most of the time. As for the trips to the fence, I have no idea what you are talking about. I will find out, though. Jamil doesn't hide anything from me.'

We were silent for a while, watching the dancers twirl

and jump again. They had so much energy. I could tell that the tallest guy there fancied the girl to his left, with whom he was holding hands as part of the choreography. Their attraction to each other radiated across the crowds and I wished I could go straight to them and offer them the use of my flat. I somehow knew they were trying to hide their love from everyone else.

'Just take care of him, Issa. Our brother is erratic – I am not sure what he is capable of. But Nouman is out to get him now and he will.' I pulled my hand away from his.

'No one will get my brother, as long as I am alive. He hasn't done anything wrong. I will go and find him now. What are you going to do? Come home with me sister, everything can be fixed.'

'No . . . I must go.'

With that, I left my brother standing among the crowds, headed towards the main road and stopped a cab.

Chapter 15

I was across the road from my flat on Talatini Road when I noticed masked men going through the front door. The security guy came out of his kiosk behind me and asked me what was happening. I said I didn't know, then asked him if I could sit down inside for a while, pretending to be tired and unable to stand. He happily obliged and brought a black leather chair for me to sit on. I thought the masked men would notice a lone woman in sunglasses standing across the street watching them. Sitting in the kiosk, I had a good view of the entrance of the building and the balcony of my flat.

To my horror, I saw the lights being switched on in my home. The men moved like shadows from one room to the next. Then they went to the back of the flat and I knew they had gone into my bedroom. What were they doing there? My heart was racing and my eyes must have been watering because the security guy asked me if I needed a glass of water. I shook my head without uttering a word and continued to stare at the flat. What had happened to my life over the last two weeks? It had all turned upside down, and to make things worse I now had strange men covered in black masks in my bedroom. For some reason I didn't care if my knickers were out in full view; in fact, I hoped they were laid out on the bed, and that one of the men might get tangled in a bra thrown on the floor, and be badly injured as a result. Imagine the headline the next morning! They would probably claim he had been injured due to a collapsed tunnel somewhere.

Then the masked men started to leave the building, taking with them several brown cardboard boxes. There were at least six of them, but I wasn't sure whether they took them from the flat or elsewhere in the building. I had never seen these boxes before, marked with the word 'Fragile' in English.

They loaded them into their jeep and drove off in a hurry. I was left there bewildered, not knowing what to do next. I was longing to go home and be in my bed. But I also knew I had started something that had to be finished. I needed to know everything and there was no way back. I was scared and unable to think what my next step should be. If only Nouman were here so I could tell him about what I had seen today; surely he would be able to tell me a little bit more about what was happening.

It was getting very cold in the kiosk. The middle-aged security guy had a small electric heater on the floor. He kept putting his hands on top of it to feel the heat, rubbing them together. I thought how lucky the UN was to always have electricity in Gaza. It was getting dark outside, and I got up, thanked my host and started walking back on Talatini Street down to University Square. The smell of falafel en route made my stomach scream with hunger, but I carried on and found a phone booth to call Um Suleiman. I rang her mobile three times but she didn't answer and she didn't have a voicemail service. I walked a little further until I got to the Ansar Area. The streets were emptying. It was a clear night and the moon was a perfect semicircle. Gaza looked like a young girl, asleep on the shores of the Mediterranean, innocent and full of youth. But this Strip was not innocent; we had made many mistakes – some terrible ones. Some people here also benefited from the occupation and the siege, and had made lots of money. You could see it in the new buildings that sprang up in the city. No one knew where they came from, but some of them were labelled as a 'Qatari Charity Project'.

I had to look for Nouman. Something must have happened to him, otherwise he would have found me by now, or sent for me at least. Some members of the Taweel family lived one street down from us on Wihda Street. Nouman had told me he lived in the Nassir area, so I had some information if I wanted to ask his family about him. How many Nouman El Taweels could there be anyway?

It was around 9 p.m. when I knocked on one of the houses. There were a few stairs leading up to the main door, beside which stood two old Ottoman pillars. There was one small lightbulb flickering in the wind, which gave the whole place a romantic look. It was the sort of place where I saw couples in movies kiss as they searched for their keys. But there was no chance of a kiss here. In fact, I didn't know what to expect, and what the family would think of this strange woman coming to ask about a man she barely knew.

A woman around my age opened the door. She was very tall; true to what seemed like family genes. She knew Nouman, of course, she explained that everyone knew him. He always came to family weddings and funerals. Being a detective meant that a lot of people contacted him when their children were arrested or accused of doing something wrong. Her name was Samia and she invited me in for a very welcome cup of tea, as I was parched. The house smelled of cooking; they had just finished their dinner. I could smell chicken and onion and guessed that they had had a *musakhan* dish – my mouth started to water.

I learned a great deal about Nouman then, how respected he was in the family and how straightforward he was. It was difficult for me to ask direct questions given that I had just turned up at her front door, but my hostess was very chatty, telling me more than I had hoped for. I asked about close relatives and friends. She told me he had many friends, but he was very close to his nephew, Alaa. She explained that the two were inseparable at most family occasions, due to the fact that Nouman had no children and Alaa's father had so many of the bastards.

'He lives down the road from here. Nouman is the only one who left this area and went to live in El Nassir. I tell you what, I'll send one of the children for him, you stay here. It's cold outside.'

'I am sorry to bother you with this.' For some reason I was about to cry. The warmth of the house, the sage tea, a woman my age talking about normal stuff as if life was just perfect – it was overwhelming. I was left alone in the guest room, as she called for one of the children to run to Alaa's house.

I was sure we had met when he walked in, his eyes were familiar. He shook Samia's hand, who then excused herself to go and put the children to bed. He looked troubled the moment he saw me, breathing quickly as he sat down on the mattress opposite me. Unlike the rest of the family, he was quite short. I was relieved to see that this wasn't a family of giants.

'*Marhaba*, how can I help you?' Alaa said sharply, as if he was in a hurry. He was surprised to be summoned to a house and to find a woman in search of his uncle.

'I am looking for your uncle, he disappeared a couple of days ago.' I don't know why I made no introductions, I just said it as it was.

'What? Disappeared! How? When?'

I started to explain, but he kept interrupting me. He wanted to know everything, but not the details I was giving. He just wanted to get to the point where Nouman left the room in Gaza's municipality building.

He immediately took a small device out of his pocket and started speaking, in what sounded to me like code. It looked like a walkie-talkie but a very advanced, small one. Then his mobile phone rang and he was talking to another person, while still carrying on the conversation on the radio device at the same time. The nephew was a Hamas Qassam Brigades fighter. I marvelled at his ability to speak to two people at the same time over the phone. Before he had finished, I heard the sound of tyres screeching outside.

'Come with me,' he said.

Samia came back, looking startled. She held her boy and girl, dressed in their pyjamas, clutching toothbrushes in their tiny hands. I smiled at them as I was led out of the house. Samia knelt down and hugged them as they all watched us leave. Outside, there were two black jeeps full of masked men. The second one had room for two. Alaa opened the door for me and ushered me in. The driver handed him a mask which he put on as soon as we got in. I had removed my sunglasses when I went into the house and was wondering whether to put them on again.

'Call Um Suleiman, now.' He handed me a mobile phone. 'We will drop you at the Omari Mosque, it is not safe to go to the municipality building.'

'What? Why? Where are you going? Where is Nouman?'

'That's what we are trying to find out! And please don't do anything else, don't speak a word to anyone apart from Um Suleiman, and don't do anything stupid. You've brought enough trouble to us already.'

His words hit me like a slap in the face. It was true, I had ruined so many people's lives, all to try to find the killer of a husband who wasn't the person I thought he was; a man who'd hardly told me anything about his life and who had pretended to be dreamy and carefree. I wished I could turn back time and forget about the whole thing. I thought how right Jamil had been when he shouted at me to give up. But it was too late now, there were people missing, I couldn't leave it anymore.

Um Suleiman was waiting in the little alley near the mosque. She looked tiny with the big arches towering behind her. She didn't say a word when I got close to her, but took my hand and led me through the main gate of the mosque and back to the same room on the right.

'I am sorry,' I said, without really knowing what I was apologising for.

She smiled. 'Don't be, you've done the right thing. I

didn't know Alaa was Qassam, how would I, if they all cover their faces? Now he will find Nouman for us, I am sure. He's his uncle and he will do his best to find him. But now, you need to get some sleep.'

She let me in with a key this time. There was no old man in a *jellabiya*. A sofa bed was set up for me with fresh sheets and towels. To my relief there was a bathroom at the end of the room, and there was also a bowl of bananas and oranges. The room smelled nice and clean and I fell asleep as soon as I got into bed.

Chapter 16

A loud bang on the door at nearly 3 a.m. woke me up. I heard shouts, and the knocking grew louder and harder. My heart sank, as I wanted nothing more than to stay in bed and bury myself under the warm duvet – I was frightened. I quickly put my headscarf on and threw my *jilbab* on top of my clothes.

A masked man fell into the room as soon as I opened the door, his shoulder bleeding badly. The other men started shouting at me to move out of the way. They laid him on the sofa bed. He was in agony, screaming like a small baby. Some other men walked in, pushing my brother Jamil, Wafa, Zakaria and Sameeh into the room. Um Suleiman followed. Finally, the man I had been searching for, Nouman, walked in, incredibly dusty and looking very tired. He was coughing a lot and looked as though he was about to collapse.

The masked men forced Jamil, Wafa, Zakaria and Sameeh to sit on the floor with their backs to the wall. They looked frightened and bewildered. A man stood next to them, pointing his gun towards them.

'Zahra!' Jamil shouted, but before he finished saying my name, the gunman kicked his left shoulder. Jamil fell on the floor, face down. I ran towards him, unable to stand the sight of my brother being beaten by an armed stranger.

'Leave him alone,' I shouted at the top of my voice, thumping the large man on his chest. He stepped back, cocked his gun and pointed it at me. All the other men turned towards us and cocked their guns in turn. I was scared for my life, of course, but I also felt powerful. I never imagined I would scare someone enough to make them raise a gun. I always thought of myself as a weak person who wouldn't even frighten an ant, but at that moment, a masked man stood in front of me, shaking, willing to shoot at any time.

'Stop!' shouted the masked man lying on the bed. He removed his mask and I saw Alaa's eyes once again, yet this time he looked much weaker, less defiant, and in a lot of pain. Nouman started walking across the room, dragging himself towards his nephew. He looked at me as he passed and gave a slight hint of a smile that made my heart fill with strange emotions – a mixture of relief, anticipation and admiration.

He sat down on the bed next to Alaa, who was screaming in agony; he held his hand tightly. His nephew looked as though he was about to burst into tears, held down by two masked men. He was in bad shape. There was a knock on the door. A young woman walked in carrying a black briefcase, dressed in jeans and a green top. She went straight to Alaa, opened her case and took out a pair of scissors. Like someone who had done this many times, she skilfully cut his black top in half. No one said a word and let her get on with her job. She spoke a very soft Arabic, giving the men orders to fetch her hot water and to keep Alaa as still as possible. She cleaned the wound and examined it, before getting out a syringe and injecting Alaa in his right arm. Within seconds, he passed out.

'I am going to operate on him now to get the bullet out of his shoulder. He has bled a lot and will need to be hospitalised soon,' she said to Nouman.

'He can't go to the hospital, not now!' Nouman responded quickly. She seemed to understand and went back to her work. Everyone was concentrating on what she was doing, no one said a word. Nouman started praying that his nephew could be saved and cursing himself for getting him into so much trouble.

He let go of Alaa's hand, and one of the masked men came and lifted him up, telling him to be strong and that Allah was going to be with him. Nouman looked away from the man towards me, and I felt the guilt of having caused all of this, hacking through my stomach like a saw. But

Nouman's expression was kind, as if he was letting me know that it wasn't my fault.

The doctor finished the last stitch, washed her hands in the bowl of hot water and put everything back in the briefcase. She dried her hands and asked the masked men to leave Alaa lying there, but to carefully change the dirty sheets. They did it with such skill, as though they had done it many times before.

'He needs to go to the hospital. That is my professional opinion.' She was talking to Nouman, but without looking at him.

'Will he survive?' Nouman pleaded.

'If he goes to hospital, yes, but if he stays here his blood pressure will drop and he will probably die in less than two hours.'

Nouman looked stressed. I could see his dilemma. If he called for an ambulance the police would ask a lot of questions. The whole thing would blow up further. If he didn't, then he would be risking his nephew's life.

'Sir,' one of the masked men said, 'we could say that he was on a Qassam mission near the Israeli border.'

'No,' I shouted immediately. Nouman looked at me, startled. But I didn't want the very same lie to be repeated again, not in my presence anyway. This lie had destroyed my life and made me go mad. I didn't want the same thing to happen to this poor guy. What if he died? Would his family also think that their son died as a martyr?'

'Okay . . . call an ambulance now. We will explain later,' he said looking at his nephew. His main concern was to get him to safety, but he was also aware he was going to be in trouble with his superiors. An unexplained, injured Qassam fighter was going to raise a lot of questions, and trouble was surely guaranteed.

'Jamil,' Nouman faced him now and looked at him directly, 'would you like to explain to your sister why you spoke to her husband just before he was killed?'

'What? I never spoke to anyone. Why am I here anyway? And what is going on?' Jamil shouted back at Nouman. Some of the masked men came closer and pointed their guns at him.

'Nouman,' I said quickly, 'please, tell them not to do this.'

'What am I doing here too?' shouted Zakaria.

'And me?' Wafa added.

'Okay, allow me to explain – given that you deserve an explanation about what is happening, and some of you are clearly in the dark regarding some of the facts. In 2014, there was a murder committed. This woman's husband, Mr. Ammar Bseiso, was killed. The murderer was very clever. To cover up the murder he put the body in a house which had just been bombed by Israel. I must say, that was well thought through. But, unfortunately, not all the tracks were covered and they made a silly mistake. This murderer is here in the room and it would save me a lot of talking if they just stepped forward and identified themselves.'

There was silence. Everyone was staring at Nouman. The masked men seemed interested too. They stared at the people sitting on the floor, who suddenly looked like defendants in a courtroom.

'So you spoke to your brother-in-law, who died an hour and a half later, and you never thought it would be worth mentioning it to your bereaved sister, even just to tell her that he was happy or sad when you spoke to him?' Nouman asked Jamil. He stared at the floor, trying to avoid meeting my eyes.

'Why? Speak please?' I screamed at my brother.

'Don't you find this strange, Mr. Jamil? Not only that; you did whatever you could to persuade your sister to stop looking for a detective who would help explore the case? Now, why was that?'

Jamil was silent, still staring at the floor, his foot shaking slightly.

'Jamil, please tell us everything. Tell us what happened?'
But he didn't respond to my pleading. His leg continued to
shake, and he avoided looking at me.

'Okay, it seems your brother has chosen the hard way of
helping us get to the truth,' Nouman said, as he looked at the
biggest masked man in the room.

'No, Nouman, please!' I couldn't see them hurt my
brother, I would never allow it. He was a bastard to me but I
could not and would not allow such a thing to happen.

Just as I spoke, we heard the sound of an ambulance and
voices on walkie-talkies. The masked men opened the door
immediately and two paramedics rushed in to pick up Alaa;
they looked puzzled to see the scene in the room. But it was
not just an ambulance which came, the medical vehicle was
followed by a police car. I assumed it was standard practice
that when someone got injured so badly like this, the police
started an investigation.

We all followed Alaa outside to the main courtyard, where
he was being loaded into the ambulance. Some masked men
stayed in the room with the prisoners. A young policeman,
who looked to be a much lower rank than Nouman, got out
of his blue police jeep and began walking towards us. My
detective did not look very happy; he was muttering under
his breath, cursing himself for not hurrying up with his
investigation.

'Well, well. What have we got here?' asked the young,
pale-faced policeman. 'It's Nouman El Taweel himself . . .
you know, we've spent the whole evening looking for you.
Where have you been?'

The masked men clenched their guns more tightly as a
big blue van arrived with police in riot gear. About fifteen
men got out and started to surround us. They pointed their
guns at the masked men and ordered them to put their
weapons down and their hands in the air. Alaa was shouting
from inside the ambulance, but no one could hear what he

was saying and Nouman didn't dare try to move closer. He was surveying the situation, looking at me and the others still sitting on the floor, the masked men and the riot police.

'Ridda, please don't do this. Leave our differences behind. This is very important and dangerous,' Nouman pleaded.

'*Habebi*, it is not me who is doing this, it is you. How could you break into a police station in Khan Younis, remove some of the prisoners against regulations, shout down your fellow police officers and then come here and tell me not to do anything? I have orders to get you by the balls, dead or alive, and you know how much I like to follow orders.'

'Yes, I know that very well. But this is different, Ridda; this is bigger than me and you. Of course, you can arrest me and take everyone in this room, but you will only earn brownie points for that, not help your country or your people.' Nouman's voice became fatherly.

'Don't patronise me with this talk please, I don't need lectures about patriotism. I was injured in the Second Intifada and nearly died,' Ridda responded sharply.

'Yes, I know, and it is for that reason I am asking you for a few moments, just half an hour or so, to finish what I'm doing. You can stay here, listen to everything and then decide for yourself.'

'Sorry, I am trying to do a job here.' Ridda smiled, a sneaky smile that was disheartening to see. He looked at his fellow officers, who started moving slowly towards the masked men, conscious they might pick up their guns again. It was my first time of seeing the police coming face to face with Qassam resistance fighters. I had always thought the latter had more authority, yet it seemed they were in trouble for doing an unauthorised job. Even though Nouman was a policeman himself, it appeared he had broken some rule, maybe because he hadn't drop my case as he was asked to do.

'How did you get out of jail, Nouman? You were there a couple of days ago. Who helped you?'

'Well, I wasn't arrested, I was under investigation as to why I hadn't dropped Mrs. Tanani's case. They kept me there for a while without offering any explanation, so I left.'

'How? That's my question,' Ridda asked, condescendingly.

'Ridda, I saved your father's life. Please, my son, just let me do this and then you can do anything you want.'

'What's going on here?' asked Ridda.

'Please Ridda, I will explain everything. Let me ask these people a few questions and then you can arrest us all if you want. You are a good man Ridda, just like your father,' Nouman pleaded again.

An awkward silence fell upon the room. I didn't know what was happening and what Nouman was referring to, but the young policeman seemed to calm down, although he still looked annoyed.

Suddenly, we heard footsteps, and I was sure I knew who it was before we had even seen them. Everyone in the room clenched their guns, ready to shoot the intruder. As the silhouette came closer, it was clear it was a masked man, my masked man, no other than Mohammed El Deif. The Hamas Qassam Brigades men recognised him immediately and so did Nouman. All lowered their guns and saluted him. The policemen looked confused, but Ridda recognised him too and he also had his hand to his forehead, saluting him.

'Let it be, Ridda.' Mohammed spoke in a loud gravelly voice. Ridda gestured to his policemen to lower their guns. When the man walked in, there was no doubt who immediately became in charge. Mohammed El Deif, the legend, had everyone captivated by his natural authority. Ridda couldn't respond to him directly, couldn't even look straight at him.

He turned towards Nouman. 'Okay, you will have twenty minutes, no more, and please don't mention my father again, God rest his soul.' Ridda's face changed, he looked kinder, less of a policeman and more like a grumpy next door neighbour.

'You heard that, Jamil, we don't have a lot of time here.

You and Ammar were far closer to each than most people realised. In fact, you had a little business together, didn't you?'

Jamil was silent. The two large policemen were still holding him by the shoulder. He looked so small next to them, dressed up in all their gear.

'Did you call Ammar to check on the business and how much money you had made that day? No, of course not! Did you tell him something that made him change where he was going? Hmm . . . maybe.'

'I did not kill anyone, I have never killed anyone!' Jamil's sense of pride and self-confidence came back to him.

'We will get to that in a minute. But first Sameeh, where were you when Ammar was killed?' Nouman asked.

'At home, there were bombs raining down on Jabalia Camp, where else would I be?' Sameeh said, matter-of-factly.

'Yes . . . yes . . . what is the saying, "Some people's problems are others' advantages"? Well, you were not at home that evening, Sameeh. Shall I say where you were? Well, we don't have a lot of time; you and Wafa were together taking a walk, not a romantic walk but walking towards El Saha to meet your best friend, Ammar Bseiso.'

I was completely perplexed. I thought Ammar didn't like Wafa, why would he be going to meet my friend without telling me? Everything was so confusing.

'You wanted the cash from him, but he didn't have it for you. He'd promised he would give you the money for the Tirmal drug you'd both been selling for some time, and that night was his final deadline.'

Sameeh was silent. He looked briefly at Wafa then stared at the floor.

'But Ammar was telling the truth, which you refused to believe. He hadn't managed to sell any boxes of the drug. Things were difficult then; there was a war on, and selling the stuff required a lot of risk on his part. He didn't want to be seen on street corners selling it in case he was mistaken for a spy giving information to Israel. So he'd been waiting for the war to finish in order to resume your little business.'

'What business are you talking about? You are not making any sense!' Sameeh shouted.

'Oh, really?' responded Nouman. 'Well, let me tell you a little story then. Once upon a time, there were three friends called Sameeh, Ammar and Jamil. Two of them are here today and the third was killed. How? With a knife – murdered by none other than his friend. Zakaria could have been the fourth friend in this underground drug cartel, but he had too much of a bad reputation already. He was known in the Camp to be a womaniser and a drunk, so the friends didn't want to risk it. They just relied on him to take them for walks near the border, relay the gossip from the Camp, tell stories about who might be potential customers for their drugs: wasted youths who had no hope in Gaza, people who wanted to forget the pain they lived in and pretend that life was okay. Zakaria knew nothing about this of course, but he inadvertently gave lots of names and useful tips. The *shisha* times in the café in Jabalia Camp were no more than market research for the business.'

'Well, why am I here then?' Zakaria interrupted.

'You were in the wrong place at the wrong time. I called the local Khan Younis Police and asked them to arrest Wafa and her husband, Mahmoud, but they got you instead. Mahmoud then made a phone call and demanded his wife was released, so I had to go and break into the prison to get you both before Wafa disappeared. You can leave now, Zakaria, if you want.'

But my old neighbour and suitor did not move, he remained where he was, staring at Nouman, surprised to hear that he was free to go. I felt bad to have put him through all of this. Everyone kept saying he had a bad reputation, but so far he was the only person to be cleared of this whole thing. He may have unwittingly given information about potential drug customers, but Zakaria didn't know what my evil husband was up to.

We caught each other's eye and I smiled, whispered 'sorry' under my breath. My eyes pleaded for forgiveness from a man who had felt so much for me, and whom I had ignored and got into so much trouble.

Jamil's eyes were fixed on Nouman, as if admiring his eloquence. As for me, I didn't really know what to feel. I was angry, relieved I wasn't deluded. But overall, I was scared to be in the company of my husband's killer, the one who made me a widow and spoiled my life forever. Even though Nouman was here and we were all surrounded by masked men and policemen with guns, I didn't feel safe. I wanted to run away to another hiding place. I was surrounded by men who did not understand what it meant to lose a husband: men who were too accustomed to war and fighting; men who believed in something that perhaps did not exist. I wanted to walk over to Nouman and tell him to shut up, that I didn't want to know who killed my bastard husband anymore, that I did not care. But it was too late; what was done could not be undone.

'One day, Sameeh came to Ammar and Jamil and proposed a little business,' Nouman continued. 'He told them he had met a beautiful woman with a strong French accent who would give them stuff to sell. Little pills that would make people in Gaza forget about the shit they were in, as Celine described it. Sameeh told Ammar and Jamil that there was no harm in it, that it was coming officially through Israel rather than the dodgy stuff through the tunnels from Egypt. He told his friends that even Hamas approved of it, because how else could it have got into Gaza other than through the Karni Crossing? They discussed it and argued, but eventually money seduced them – all but one. The brother-in-law was too fearful of the outcome, he was too worried about his sister, and above all he genuinely believed it was a bad idea, that selling drugs which came through the people who occupied and besieged us was a very bad idea.'

I looked at my brother, who was about to burst into tears. He was crouched on the floor rocking backwards and forwards, muttering inaudibly under his breath.

'But the two other friends agreed to do it for a while, to make some money and then leave Gaza. What was the harm in it anyway? Sameeh and Ammar started to believe that they were doing us – the ordinary, unintelligent public – a service. Didn't you, Sameeh?'

There was an anger in Nouman's voice that I hadn't heard before. He wasn't just mad at them, but also repulsed by their actions.

'Sameeh convinced Ammar to keep going to Jabalia Camp and to strengthen his friendship with Jamil, who could introduce him to the locals, help them familiarise themselves with the area and find a good spot in the north where the exchange of goods could happen and where Celine could cross easily. Ammar left it for a few months and then asked Jamil to do exactly that. He made sure to persuade Jamil that he and Sameeh had given up on the idea of selling drugs. They never talked about it again. Your brother, Zahra, is not as clever as he would like to think. He introduced Ammar to Abu Eyyad, took him to his farm, saw an exchange of goods once, but did not connect the two together. He did not realise Ammar had already started the business of selling illegal drugs – those Tirmal pills.

'Now, where does Wafa fit in all of this? Well, she was the business development person, spreading word through her network and taking orders for Sameeh and Ammar to deliver.

'They would get the boxes from Abu Eyyad's farm in El Soudaniya, load them on a donkey cart, cover them with some hay bales and go through Gaza unnoticed. But when the war started, Ammar wasn't able to sell anything. He had to move the boxes from their normal hiding place in Firas Market to his flat, when Zahra wasn't home. It was too risky to leave them there with all the bombardment. But Sameeh and Wafa didn't believe his story and asked for their share of the sale. They met in a car park to talk about it, in El Saha, on the heaviest night of bombing ever. An argument broke out. Sameeh got out a knife and stabbed Ammar. He died instantly. They panicked, not knowing what to do. Surely, someone had seen them together. Wafa suggested putting Ammar's body in Sameeh's car.

'They drove off without knowing what to do. They went through Shujaia and saw people were fleeing as the news came through that Israel was invading the area to try and find their kidnapped soldiers. They saw a house that had just been hit, smoke coming out of it. The street was empty and dark, they both got out, dragged the body into the house, left it there and took off.

'When I read the coroner's report, Zahra had already told me that Ammar was the only person in the house with a stab wound. But what Zahra didn't know was that her husband's body was the only one to have scratches, after being dragged along the floor. Also, in the pictures taken at the scene, Ammar's body was the only one on top of the rubble, whereas the others were buried underneath, hardly visible if you didn't know they were there. He was the first one to be sent to the morgue according to the report, the others followed two hours later, after rescue teams worked hard to retrieve their bodies.

'Also, the time of death was different to the others – that's when I believed you, Zahra'.

I collapsed on the floor; it was too much. I hadn't known all of that, and somehow I felt very stupid for not digging deeper into it, for not even reading the report properly or demanding an explanation. Everything had happened at the same time. The war had continued, the grief had grown bigger, the sense of loss had been so disorienting that I hadn't gone into that much detail. I was convinced my husband had been murdered; it was an instinct more than a conclusion based on any sort of calculation. I was right, but knowing those details would have been handy: maybe I would have found a detective quicker; maybe I wouldn't have gone all around Gaza like a crazy woman; maybe my family would have believed me straight away, or even better, Jamil would've come forward much earlier and saved me and everyone else all of this hassle.

I looked at Sameeh and Wafa. She had her head down and didn't say a word. Zakaria's eyes were blazing.

'You have no proof,' Sameeh said quickly.

'Well, you can check the story with Jamil. Ammar phoned him before he died, remember? He confessed everything to him. He told him he was going to meet you two and talk about the money. He also said he was worried for his life. Jamil tried to convince him not to go and offered to go up to El Saha to meet with you. The trouble was that Jamil couldn't do this right then, as he was in the middle of a battlefield fighting an Israeli invasion, along with his friends in El Qassam Brigades in Jabalia Camp. He would not have been able to get out. So this confirms you were meeting with the deceased at exactly the time of his death, as the post mortem confirmed. Now, I don't want to pretend that I'm clever or anything, but surely you can see where I am going with this. Oh, and one more thing actually, a little security camera on the main gate of the car park shows that the three of you walked past there at exactly 6:27 p.m. – just half an hour before Ammar was killed.

Jamil was shocked to hear that the business had carried on, because he truly believed the idea had been dropped. He didn't have any reason not to believe his brother-in-law and his friend. He didn't know what to do when Ammar confessed to him on the night of the murder. The next day, when he learned of your husband's death, Zahra, he didn't know how to respond. The only thing he did was to tell your mother everything and try to stop you from investigating it, believing that it made no difference how Ammar died, as he was still dead at the end of it all. Your mother made me promise not to arrest him for obstructing justice when I interviewed her. And like Jamil, the only thing your mother could do was to keep silent and hope you would fail to find a detective, hope that the possibility of someone crazy looking into this case was very remote, that everything would settle down sooner or later. Your mum said she had intended to tell you. But not then, she wanted time to wash away all this pain.'

I couldn't speak a word, a mixture of anger and disappointment with Wafa and Sameeh paralysed me completely. How dare Sameeh be the one to inform me of the death of my husband. Why did he even tell me? Did he have no humanity left? He killed his closest friend, and when his friend's wife called him the next day he pretended to know nothing, only to ring her back later to break the news of the death. He presented it to her as a simple fact – the death which himself was responsible for.

'And you, Wafa, I thought we were friends. You lied to me, you went out to look for a detective with me while knowing exactly who had killed Ammar. Why? What the hell?'

I got up and started shouting at Wafa, I wanted to grab her by the hair and drag her across the floor. Nouman saw me heading towards her and stopped me before I got to her.

'Don't blame her – well, not too much. She was involved, of course, but not out of choice. She was forced to do it. Wafa's husband, Mr. Mahmoud El Astal, the conservative guy who pretended to be a saint, was no more than a Tirmal drug trader. A big one too, very powerful and well connected to the government I'm afraid. In fact, one of the biggest importers in Gaza, this is why half of our youth are drugged all the time.

'The trouble with the little plot Ammar and Sameeh had going was that they didn't realise how quickly news spreads in Gaza about the new kids on the block selling pills. Wafa's husband made a few phone calls and found out one of the two friends selling drugs was the husband of his wife's best friend, Zahra. What a coincidence! This solved the problem for him. Instead of trying to confront the two to get them to stop trading, he thought of a better plan. He forced his wife to be part of the gang and share the profit, getting easy money without having to do anything. He even gave Wafa some contacts for her to sell to. How else do you think an educated woman with a first-class English degree would know drug dealers in Gaza? Well, she didn't, he gave her all the contacts. He beat her up several times, threatened to take the children away and throw her in prison if she didn't comply. Eventually, she did, she had no other choice. Well, she did, in my opinion, but let's not go there.'

I looked at Mohammed El Deif, who was listening intently, his eyes gleaming behind his mask. But for some reason I felt he knew everything Nouman was saying. There was something about the way he looked at the person Nouman was about to address before my detective even started speaking. Maybe I was just imagining this, but having spent so much time with him in my hiding place, I felt I could read his eyes well. I was the only one he had revealed his face to, by mistake to start with, but then by choice. He didn't remove it in that big scene, he didn't trust anyone but me.

'Wafa went to see Sameeh one day in Gaza City,' Nouman carried on 'They went to Delice Café and she told him she knew all about his business with Ammar. She threatened to go to the police and tell them everything if they didn't let her join in. Sameeh told Ammar and they both decided they had no other option but to get her involved as well. This is how the ring was formed. The three musketeers then tried to recruit Jamil, who thought better of it and declined the offer. Mind you, it was only meant to be a one-off then, a quick money-spinner. But Jamil wouldn't take part. Jamil is part of the Qassam Brigades; he is a true patriot and fighter. He is not interested in money, he is interested in freedom and Palestine more than anything. Mahmoud El Astal was their pimp, if you like; he was the most powerful, yet the invisible partner in all of this. This is why I was asked to drop the case by my superiors, because he had connections, and you, Zahra, were stupid enough to tell your friend everything about the investigation. Why do you think she came to stay with you for a week?

'Wafa was giving her husband and Sameeh information about you, Zahra, and how far you'd got with finding a detective. He followed you once and even took the trouble to break into your house in Jabalia Camp, thinking he could kill two birds with one stone – find out what you had come up with and see how much Jamil was involved.

'And how did they start trading? Hmm, well this is the interesting part. Your French friend Celine is not French and not called Celine either. When you gave me that picture of her, I asked friends who had contacts in the Border Control Police, and they matched it with an Israeli girl who had entered Gaza twice at the beginning of the Oslo Agreement, when Fatah was in power. Her name is Yvette Aaronvich. She had pretended to be an American exchange student at the time and came to Gaza to do some work for Mossad. Yes, she is a Mossad agent. Now the only thing that I can't say is whether she kept in touch with Ammar from the time they first met or not. But I am sure that the second time they met, they would have recognised each other. How did Yvette come into contact with Sameeh? I don't know, but I am sure we will find out by the end of this. Won't we, Sameeh?'

Ridda was staring at Nouman in bewilderment; he had calmed down now and was listening intently to everything. I heard the loud buzzing of a drone flying close to us, it was an Israeli one – the sound of which was too familiar to us in Gaza. We had become accustomed to the sound of those faceless machines at the start of the second Intifada in 2000. Whenever we heard the buzzing, we knew there was a bomb to follow. They had become part of our lives ever since, taking images of everything on the street, inside our houses, in our living rooms and bedrooms, in cafés, at work and everywhere we walked. Some people believed that the Israelis knew all details about us, including how many times we made love a week. But not about this man, Mohammed, the Guest. He was a shadow, he knew how to avoid all of the spies, all of the drones, soldiers, cameras and even our own Palestinian traitors who might be seduced by the reward over his head too. Did he make a mistake that evening? Was the drone I was hearing sent to track him down? He didn't seem to be concerned though. He had his own way of intelligence too, he knew who to trust and how to operate underground. The Qassam Brigades also started developing their own intelligence, albeit on a low scale in comparison to the mighty Israeli Mossad. But Mohammed, my Guest, had no bodyguards or anyone protecting him. Perhaps that was his power, blending casually, like any other person, maybe he used make up to disguise his appearance when walking down the streets, or going to a falafel restaurant. Or maybe he simply kept his mask on and walked freely like any other Hamas fighter. Who would know the difference?

'How do I know all of this?' Nouman's voice snapped me out of my thoughts. 'Well, we have already established that Wafa and Sameeh were with Ammar on the night of his death. I was shocked to learn this to start with, given that Zahra had told me the friends had lost touch and were not close anymore, that the friendship circle was broken. It turned out it wasn't, it was just that business was conducted elsewhere, not in the flat. I put a tailgate on Wafa to watch her movements, and noticed she and Sameeh had met twice in the last couple of weeks. I also asked a policeman to follow Sameeh's movements and he went to the border only five days ago and met with Yvette, or Celine, if you would like to call her that. My source told me there was a lot of shouting and that she had pulled a gun on him. I had to act fast before Sameeh, or anyone else in this gang, got killed too. We had to keep a close eye on the border. I was sure Yvette would come back again. Alaa got his Qassam men and we went the day after to the border and waited. Sure enough, she turned up. She lingered near the beach and I walked over. She was expecting to see Sameeh and was shocked to see me. I dressed up just like him so she couldn't tell the difference from a distance. It didn't take her long to confess everything after I put a gun to her head. I wanted to arrest her too and hand her over to the resistance. She would've been a marvellous gift to them – a Mossad agent in the hands of the resistance would be of great value. She would have been worth at least another thousand Palestinian prisoners being released from Israeli prisons.

'But something happened, and an Israeli military jeep turned up. She must have sent a message. They started shooting and I nearly got killed. Alaa and his men started firing to give me cover and I retreated – we all survived but it could've turned nasty and perhaps started a new war.

'Then I had to find Wafa and Sameeh. I sent a message to the local police at Khan Younis and asked them to arrest Wafa and her husband about three days ago. The next day, I was arrested myself for not following the order to drop the case. Wafa's husband pulled some strings and put me in jail instead. It wasn't until you went to see Alaa that he figured everything out, made a few phone calls and realised I was being held in El Saraya prison. He broke in with his men and got me out. We drove all the way to Khan Younis and now here we are . . .'

'Are you sure about all of this?' Ridda interrupted

Nouman.

'I have a recording of the whole of Yvette's confession, my old friend. Now please, I am not the one you should arrest. Ridda, you need to arrest Mahmoud El Astal and a few powerful people in government. Please, I beg you'. Nouman handed a USB stick to the young policeman. 'Here, everything about the case, including evidence, is on there.'

Nouman then walked slowly towards Jamil and Zakaria and started pulling them up to their feet. The masked men continued to point their guns at Wafa and Sameeh.

Seeing my brother freed was very emotional. I felt so bad for having suspected him, for being angry with him, for not listening to what he said. I wanted to run to him and give him a big hug, but I knew, being such a conservative guy, he wouldn't appreciate it in front of all these people. Instead, I backed away from him, hoping he would come to me in the corner of the room. I kept on retreating until I bumped into the little kitchenette in the corner. I leant against it and saw Nouman and Ridda chatting and laughing, but couldn't tell what it was all about. I put my hand behind my back to support myself and felt something sharp. I looked around and there was a big kitchen knife lying there. I held it for a moment, staring at it. I glanced up to see Jamil looking back at me, shaking his head as if he knew what was going through mine. He was telling me not to put my thoughts into action, but without further consideration I charged forward with all my energy, like a bull chasing a red rag.

Nouman saw me, and within a second he had intercepted me, rugby-tackling me to the floor. The knife fell away from me as everyone looked towards us, stunned to see us both on the ground. The police and Qassam Brigades quickly ran towards Sameeh and arrested him, someone else ran towards the knife and took hold of it.

'No, I want you to be alive and free, not rotting in some prison, or even worse, hanged for murder – enough blood.'

I started crying and pushed him away from me. He purposely fell on his back, a tired man taking a rest. He stayed lying next to me as I carried on crying.

The door was pushed open, and the police and fighters cocked their guns. Issa came running in and stopped in the middle of the room as soon as he saw me lying on the floor. Jamil walked up to him and gave him a big hug.

I looked towards where Mohammed had been sitting, but he'd gone. I could almost trace his shadow to where he'd been. The Shadow, the Guest, El Dief, the one and only, had disappeared. Just like that. And I knew then I would never see him again and no one would ever believe I'd met him, even if I told people everything that had happened. No one would believe that a man of his stature would be working as a guard somewhere in the municipality building, or that he could move to Khan Younis so quickly and arrive at my destination before me.

Chapter 17

Mother came to visit me on the 10th January 2017, three days later. She sat on the sofa in my flat as I went to prepare lunch. She hadn't spoken to me since she learned the whole story from Jamil and Issa, and I didn't feel like calling her the day after. In a way, I wanted her to call and apologise for not trusting me, for not believing in me. But being right meant that I was also wrong. I was the one who chose Ammar, who fought for him, who led a different life – only to discover my husband was a crook. How could I face her with all of this? To shout at her and yet ask for her forgiveness, and to tell her she was right at the same time? I had chosen the wrong man, and perhaps the wrong life altogether.

The doorbell rang; Um Suleiman came in as I opened the door and gave me a big hug. She joined Mother on the sofa while I returned to the kitchen to increase the portions of the humous plates I was preparing with pickles and pitta bread.

We moved to the dinner table, and to start with we ate in silence.

'How is Nouman?' asked Mother, to my surprise.

'He is okay, he is coming round for lunch to ours this Friday. He said he was busy with lots of paperwork and reports he had to produce for Ridda. It caused a stir after the police arrested all the top officials involved in the case. Hamas is trying to keep it quiet but there has been a leak to the general public, so they'd like to get everything done and dusted as quickly as possible'

'And Alaa? How is he?' I asked.

'He is in hospital still, he is recovering well but still in a lot of pain.' Um Suleiman answered.

We were eating and chatting, three women of different generations, different struggles and different pain. For a moment something felt bitter, the fact we hadn't trusted each other at some point, or maybe it was not knowing where to go from there. With the truth revealed I wasn't sure what I had left to look forward to.

'I want to thank you for looking after my daughter, Um Suleiman.' Mother was tearful. Um Suleiman got up and hugged her in return and I found myself crying.

***

The next day I went to El Shiffa Hospital to check on Alaa. He was asleep when I arrived at his room. I left the flowers next to his bed and headed for the door, but I stopped dead as I saw Nouman watching me while stretching both hands on the door frame.

'You know flowers are not allowed here? Someone could be allergic?'

'Really? Since when has this rule been in place?' I asked, genuinely concerned. But Nouman smiled and started walking towards me. I wanted to run to him and hug him, kiss him straight on the lips, but I thought better of it. I was overcome with shyness, my cheeks blazed red and I couldn't look at his beautiful face.

'Would I be out of line if I invited you for a coffee, now I am not your detective anymore?' he asked me, still smiling.

'I don't know what Hamas would say about that?' I responded.

'Well, my superiors would be completely against it. It's against any professional guidelines. But I don't care.'

We walked out of the door in silence and carried on until we arrived at Delice Café, opposite the hospital. After taking a sip of my cappuccino, I finally managed to look straight at Nouman. I was feeling more relaxed.

'Did you actually believe my story when I first walked into your office?'

'No,' he said quickly, without any hesitation. I was shocked with this abrupt answer.

'Oh.'

'But I did when you left. There was a look on your face which gave me the impression you were telling the truth, or at least you believed in what you were saying.'

I wanted him to carry on, but he stopped. I wanted to know what I looked like during those days of being so lost and confused.

'How are you feeling now?' he asked.

'Well, I am still collecting all the pieces together. I feel like a part of me has been restored, that now I know the truth I'm a broken vase which has been plastered back together. Yet the cracks in this vase are painful. All the deception and lying is so dizzying. Sometimes I just have to lie down.'

'It will take some time. What about us? Where do we go from here?'

The question shocked me. Really? Did I understand this correctly? Was he actually saying what I thought he was saying?

But yes, where would we go from here? We couldn't just go out together as boyfriend and girlfriend. He was older than me and everyone knew he was my detective. I wasn't sure if I wanted to get married again, or whether he wanted to. In that moment, I felt like running away and forgetting about everything.

I looked at him and his face lit up. He also appeared nervous, and for the first time I felt he was more vulnerable than I had ever been in front of him. How had he hidden all his feelings before?

What would Mother, Jamil and Isaa say about me marrying my detective, a man in his fifties?

I looked around nervously. The waiter was taking

someone else's order at the other side of the café and had his back to us. I reached out for Nouman's hand, which was resting on the table, pulled it down onto my lap and held it tightly. He smiled and so did I, and at that moment we were both relaxed and aroused, yet still anxious and vulnerable – all our feelings clearly etched on our faces. Yet nothing mattered then, not the society around us, my family, my dead husband, the age difference, whether we were going to get married or not – we both looked at each other and knew we wanted to cherish this moment and make it last as long as possible. Everything else could be worked out later.

Acknowledgements

There are many people to thank for their support of this work. In particular I would like to assert my appreciation to my five sisters who became my focus group, discussing difficult issues covered in this novel with an open mind. Themes like, gender equality, sexuality and class issues were the subject of many debates over the phone and when I visited Gaza a few times since starting to write this novel. I would also like to thank many friends in Gaza who also helped me sharpen the female voice of Zahra. Special thanks goes to Alaa Massood, Sama Abu Mattar, Fatma Dar Nour and Asmaa Ayash.

I would also like to thank many friends in London who have enabled me to write this work and gave valuable feedback. I would like to specifically thank Souraya Ali for her amazing editorial input, Jasr Kawkaby for letting me use his house as a writing room, Tania Khalil and Myriam Sauter for all the creative discussions we've had and my wife Heather Gardner for being so patient while I finished the book.

This book is a work of fiction and should be read as such.

Ahmed Masoud

Biography

Ahmed Masoud is the author of the acclaimed novel *Vanished: The Mysterious Disappearance of Mustafa Ouda*. Ahmed is a writer and director who grew up in Palestine and moved to the UK in 2002. In 2019, he worked with Maxine Peake on *Obliterated*, a theatrical experiment and artistic protest - you can find a small piece on Youtube.

Ahmed's Theatre and Radio Drama credits include: *Application 39* (WDR Radio, Germany 2018) *Camouflage* (London 2017), *The Shroud Maker* (London 2015 – still touring), *Walaa, Loyalty* (London 2014, funded by the Arts Council England), *Escape from Gaza* (BBC Radio 4 2011). Ahmed is the founder of Al Zaytouna Dance Theatre (2005 – 2013) where wrote and directed many productions with subsequent tours in the UK and Europe, including *Unto the Breach* (London and Vienna 2012) *Between the Fleeting Words* (London, Zurich, Freiburg, Ljubljana, Madrid 2010 – 2012). *Ila Haif* (London, Freiburg 2008-2010) *Hassad* (London 2007-2008). After finishing his PhD research, Ahmed published many journals and articles including a chapter in the Britain and Muslim World: A Historical Perspective (Cambridge Scholars Publishing, 2011). Most recently, Ahmed launched his new artistic initiative called PalArt Collective. For more information, please see www.ahmedmasoud.co.uk